Blood Feud

ALSO BY ALYXANDRA HARVEY

My Love Lies Bleeding

Blood Feud

ALYXANDRA HARVEY

BLOOMSBURY

LONDON BERLIN NEW YORK SYDNEY

First published in Great Britain in July 2010 by Bloomsbury Publishing Plc
36 Soho Square, London WID 3QY

First published in the USA in July 2010 by Walker Publishing, Inc
175 Fifth Avenue, New York, NY 10010

A CIP catalogue record of this book is available from the British Library

ISBN 978 I 4088 0705 7

FSC
Mixed Sources
Product group from well-managed
forests and other controlled sources
Cert no. SGS - COC - 2061
www.fsc.org
© 1996 Forest Stewardship Council

Printed in Great Britain by Clays Ltd, St Ives plc, Bungay, Suffolk

5 7 9 10 8 6

www.bloomsbury.com/childrens
www.alyxandraharvey.com

For Pat, who suggested to a bored nine-year-old me:
"Why don't you write a story?"

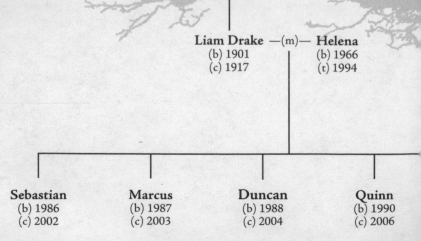

THE DRAKE FAMILY TREE

Jason Drake —(m)— **Gwyneth Llewellyn**
(b) 1613   (b) 1635
(c) 1629   (t) 1661

Edward Drake —(m)— **Hyacinth**
(b) 1789   (b) 1857
(c) 1805   (t) 1887
(d) 1914

Liam Drake —(m)— **Helena**
(b) 1901   (b) 1966
(c) 1917   (t) 1994

Sebastian   **Marcus**   **Duncan**   **Quinn**
(b) 1986   (b) 1987   (b) 1988   (b) 1990
(c) 2002   (c) 2003   (c) 2004   (c) 2006

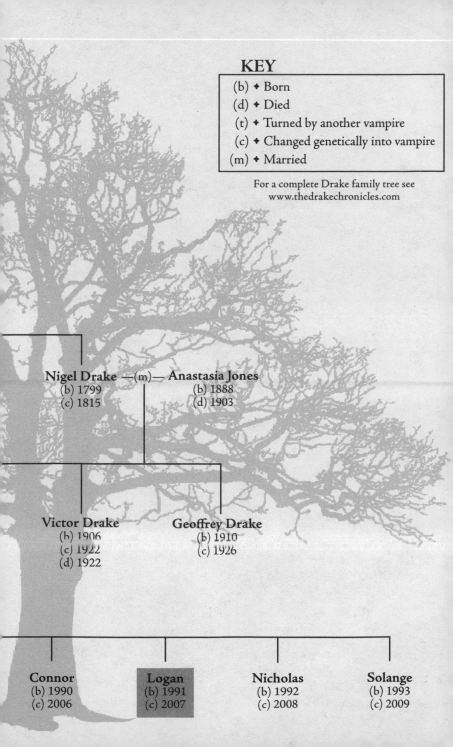

KEY

(b) ✦ Born
(d) ✦ Died
(t) ✦ Turned by another vampire
(c) ✦ Changed genetically into vampire
(m) ✦ Married

For a complete Drake family tree see
www.thedrakechronicles.com

Nigel Drake —(m)— **Anastasia Jones**
(b) 1799   (b) 1888
(c) 1815   (d) 1903

Victor Drake
(b) 1906
(c) 1922
(d) 1922

Geoffrey Drake
(b) 1910
(c) 1926

Connor
(b) 1990
(c) 2006

Logan
(b) 1991
(c) 2007

Nicholas
(b) 1992
(c) 2008

Solange
(b) 1993
(c) 2009

Blood
Feud

PROLOGUE

England, 1795

If Isabeau St. Croix had known it was going to be her last Christmas Eve, she would have had a third helping of plum pudding.

As it was, she was avoiding the drawing rooms. She'd never imagined a parlor could be so crowded and stuffy, but when she'd mentioned it to Benoit, he'd only laughed and told her to wait for summer, when coal fog clogged the city.

"Don't think I don't see you there, *chou*," he remarked dryly. He was tall and thin with a dashing mustache. So many fine gentlemen had fled France during the Revolution that every fine house in London now boasted a French chef. Never mind that most of those chefs had never even learned to boil an egg at home. They certainly did well enough here. "*Mais non*, you are murdering my carrots." He shooed away one of his harried helpers.

Taking advantage of his momentary distraction, Isabeau shrank back into the shadows of the bustling kitchen. She ought to have known better. Benoit was determined to have her dancing in satin slippers, as any nobleman's daughter would. Not too long ago she would have begged for the chance. And before that she would have expected it.

Spending a year on the streets of Paris had changed her.

Silk dresses and pearl earbobs seemed decadent now, and the concerns of fashion and gossip ridiculous. Benoit despaired that she preferred his company to the opera. But she loved the crackling of the hearth, the heavy scents of baking bread and roasting meat. Tonight there were bowls of oysters, plates of foie gras, a turkey stuffed with chestnuts, almond cream, and tiny perfect pastries in the shape of suns and holly leaves.

Benoit was the only person she could truly talk to. Her uncle was kind enough, as was his wife, but he hadn't lived in France for nearly two decades. Benoit had lived in Paris during the storming of the Bastille. He knew. But he still wasn't going to let her hide out in the kitchen all night, no matter how she begged.

"One little slice of galette." He handed her a plate and a fork. It was a traditional Galette des Rois, served in every French house during the holidays. She took a greedy bite. The second mouthful revealed the hidden dry bean tucked into the cake. She sucked the filling off it and dropped it onto her plate.

"Voilà!" Benoit grinned. "I knew you would get the bean. Now you are queen for the night." He plucked the fork from her hand even though she protested. She hadn't finished scraping every grain of sugar off the silver tines. "And so you must dance until dawn. *Allez-y!*"

She slid off a wooden stool, knowing she couldn't avoid the festivities any longer. It would be rude of her, and she had every reason to be grateful to her uncle. It hadn't been easy for her to steal enough money for the passage to England and he could have turned her away when she reached his doorstep. He'd never even met her, after all; she was the daughter of his estranged brother. His dead estranged brother, who hadn't spoken to him since before Isabeau was born. And if it wasn't for her uncle Olivier, or Oliver St. Cross as he was known here, she'd be spending this Christmas the same as she'd spent the last: huddled under the eaves of a cafe hoping some *citoyen* might give in to the holiday spirit and buy her a meal. If not, she'd have nicked the coins from someone's pocket and bought it for herself. One learned to do as one must while living in the alleys of Paris during the Great Terror.

"*Allez, allez,*" Benoit urged her. "I insist you find some handsome young man to flirt with you."

She couldn't imagine any young man would notice her, even in the beautiful white silk gown she'd been given to wear. She still felt skinny and hungry and smudged with dirt and hadn't the vaguest notion how to dance anymore. She had confidence only in her abilities to steal food and to find the best rooftops on which to hide when the riots broke out.

She forced herself to leave the kitchen mostly because the thought of the dozens of guests upstairs terrified her so. Before Paris, she had lived on a grand family estate in the countryside.

The house had marble floors and silk settees and dusty vineyards where she could eat grapes until her fingers turned purple. But then her parents had been taken.

What was a Christmas ball to the threat of the guillotine?

She found her way to the drawing room, where the guests had gathered for the midnight supper. Her uncle had leaped at the chance to re-create his own favorite childhood memories of *Réveillon* under the guise of making his niece more comfortable. He wasn't fooling anyone. They could all see how thrilled he was to be serving tourtiere and champagne to his friends. He stood by the main hearth, which was draped with evergreen branches and white lilies from the hothouse. His waistcoat was holly-berry red, barely containing his cheerful girth.

"Ah, here she is," he said.

Isabeau concentrated on smiling, on not tripping on the hem of her gown and not wiping her sweaty palms on her skirts, on anything but the curious and pitying eyes tracking her progress. "My niece, Lady Isabeau St. Croix," her uncle announced. In Paris she had introduced herself as Citoyenne Isabeau. It was safer.

"Oh, my dear," an old woman fluttered at her, the ostrich feather in her hair bobbing sympathetically. "How awful. How perfectly awful."

"*Madame.*" She didn't know what else to say to that, so she curtsied.

"Those barbarians," she continued. "Never mind that now, you're quite safe here. We English know the natural order of things."

Another sentence she had no reply for. The woman seemed

genuine, though, and she smelled like peppermint oil. Her satin gloves were trimmed with red bows when she patted Isabeau's hand. "My nephew is around here somewhere, I'm certain he would love to partner you in a dance."

"*Merci, madame.*" She had every intention of hiding behind one of the giant evergreen displays before succumbing to any such fate.

The drawing room was even more beautiful than Isabeau could have imagined. She had helped set out the bowls of gilded pine cones and holly leaves dusted with silver and tied the ribbons around the pine boughs fastened to every window. But at night, with dozens of beeswax candles burning and the frigid winter wind pushing at the glass, it was magical. And just as stuffy as she had feared, thanks to the hot air laced with cloying perfumes and floral hair oils filling every corner of the room. She edged toward the doors leading out to the gardens.

The rosebushes and yew hedges were edged with a delicate frost, as if lace had been tossed everywhere. The moon was a soft glow behind thick clouds. She shivered a little when snow began to fall gently, but didn't go back inside. She could hear icy carriage wheels creaking from the road and the sounds of music from the room behind her. The snow made everything pale as a pearl. She smiled.

"With a smile like that, I forbid you ever to frown again."

She whirled at the voice, shoulders tensing. She'd only been living in the pampered townhouse for a little while and already she was losing her edge. She ought to have heard his footsteps, or at least the door opening.

"Forgive my intrusion," he said smoothly, bowing. "And my impertinence, seeing as we have yet to be properly introduced. But you could only be the mysterious Isabel St. Cross."

"Isabeau," she corrected him softly. She'd never known a man like him. He only looked to be in his twenties, but he carried himself with an elegance and a confidence of one much older. His eyes were gray, nearly colorless in the winter garden.

"Philip Marshall, Earl of Greyhaven, at your service." When he kissed the back of her hand, his touch was cool, as if he'd been standing in the snow too long. She was suddenly nervous and felt inexplicably trapped, like the time she'd been caught behind a fire set in the streets to keep the city guards at bay.

"I should return," she murmured. She was only eighteen years old, after all, and the only reason she'd been permitted to attend the ball was because it was Christmastime. It was probably unseemly for her to be outside unchaperoned, even if he was an earl. She couldn't remember. Her aunt had listed off so many rules, they were bleeding together. She'd known them all before the Revolution. Now she only knew she felt an odd desire to stand closer to him, and not just because she had forgotten her wrap inside.

He released her hand, arched an eyebrow. The faint light from the parlor glinted on the silver buttons of his brocade coat. "Surely a girl who survived the French mobs isn't afraid of me?"

She lifted her chin defensively.

"*Mais non, monsieur. Je n'ai pas peur.*" She had to concentrate to speak English; temper or distraction always slipped her back into French. "*Pardon.*" She shook her head, annoyed with her lapse. "I am not afraid."

"I'm glad to hear it," he approved. "Wine?" He handed her a glass she hadn't realized he was holding. Hadn't Benoit been pushing her to dance and flirt? Normal girls her age would be thrilled to be standing here with a handsome earl. She should drink and eat candied violets and dance until her satin slippers wore thin. She accepted the cup.

"*Merci, monsieur.*" The mulled wine was warm and laced with cinnamon and some other indefinable taste, like copper or liquorice. Or blood. She frowned inwardly. She was letting her misgivings make her silly.

"You are lovely," he said. "And I am so tired of these English roses, too meek to enjoy anything but the quadrille and weak lemonade. You are a welcome change, Miss Cross. A welcome change indeed."

She blushed. The wine was making her feel warm, befuddled. It was nice. Snowflakes landed on her eyelashes, dissolved instantly. They landed on her lips and she licked at them as if they were sugar. His silvery eyes glinted like animal eyes, like a fox in a henhouse.

"If this were a gothic novel," he drawled, "there would be ghosts and vampires, and you *would* be afraid."

She thought of the books she read late at night in the library, sensationalist novels like Ann Radcliffe's *Mysteries of Udolpho* and Burger's *Lenore*, all fraught with villains and undead creatures who roamed the nights with insatiable appetites.

"Don't be silly." She laughed. "I don't believe in vampires."

Chapter 1

Logan

It had been a hell of a week.

Cleaning up after a psychotic vampire queen wasn't easy at the best of times. It was much worse when your mother was the one who'd dispatched the old queen, you and your brothers were suddenly princes, and your baby sister was being stalked by a centuries-old homicidal vampire.

Like I said, hell of a week.

At least we'd all survived, even Aunt Hyacinth, whose face was now so scarred she wouldn't lift the veil off her Victorian hat or leave her room. Helios-Ra vampire hunters did that to her—right before one of their new agents started dating my baby sister.

That's just weird.

Still, he saved her life less than two weeks ago, so we're willing to overlook a little making out.

As long as I never, ever have to know about it.

I mean, sure, Kieran's a good enough guy—but Solange is my only sister. Enough said.

"Quit brooding, Lord Byron." My brother Quinn smirked at me, shoving me with his shoulder. "There are no girls here to impress with your Prince of Darkness routine."

"As if." Quinn was the one who used the whole vampire mystique thing to get the girls. I just happened to like dressing in old frock coats and pirate shirts; that some girls liked it was incidental. Well, mostly.

"Any word yet on the Hound princess?" Quinn asked.

"Nothing yet." Dad had invited the reclusive Hound tribe to the table for negotiations now that Mom was the new vampire queen, ruler of all the disparate tribes. Sounds melodramatic and medieval, but that's a vampire for you.

"Think she's cute?"

"Aren't they all?"

Quinn grinned. "Mostly."

The royal caves behind us had been left in shambles after the battle that took out Lady Natasha. The dust of staked vampires was swept up and the shards of broken mirrors carted out in boxfuls. There were still at least a dozen left hanging on the wall. Lady Natasha had really liked looking at herself. Some of the ravens carved on her whitethorn throne were chipped, some decapitated. Everyone was busy with some task or another, cleaning, arranging, or just staring at my mother as she sat at the end of the hall scowling at my father, who wouldn't stop talking about peace treaties.

The tension vibrating the air was harder to clean out than the ashes of our dead.

Everyone was watching their backs: the old royalists loyal to Lady Natasha, the ones loyal to the House of Drake and my mother, and the ones caught in between. Lucy would have been running around with white sage chanting some Vedic mantra to cleanse our auras if she were here. But she was forbidden to come to the caves until the worst of the politics had been sorted out. She shouldn't have been staying with us either, but her parents' drive home was interrupted by their ancient van and some ancient part that fell out on the highway. They were stuck in a small town and Lucy was stuck with us. Humans were fragile at the best of times, and Solange's best friend didn't have the basic self-preservation of a gnat. If there was trouble, she always jumped right in feetfirst. If she hadn't started it in the first place, of course.

Between her and my sister, we had our hands full. Vampire politics paled in comparison.

"Now *she's* cute," Quinn murmured appreciatively as one of the courtiers dragged a box of what looked like the remains of a broken table. "I'll just go help her out. It's the princely thing to do."

"You're an ass," I told him fondly.

"You're just jealous because I'm so much prettier," he tossed out over his shoulder as he left to charm yet another girl.

He never reached her.

She straightened suddenly, stepping onto a footstool that gave her a good view of the length of the hall, and my parents in particular. She pulled a crossbow loaded with three wickedly pointed stakes out of the bag.

Not a broken table after all.

And no matter how prepared you are, or how careful, there's always an opening somewhere.

Mom taught us that.

The girl aimed and squeezed the trigger, barely making a sound. We might not even have noticed her at all if we hadn't been actively watching her. The stakes hissed out of the crossbow, hurtling through the air with deadly accuracy.

Or what would have been deadly accuracy had Quinn not been close enough to grab her leg and yank her off the stool.

The shot went wide, but not quite wide enough. She tumbled to the hand-embroidered rug, Quinn's fangs extending so fast they caught the lamplight. My own stung my gums, my lips lifting off the rest of my teeth.

I didn't have time to reach her or my parents.

I only had time enough to whip the dagger at my belt out into the trajectory of the stakes. It caught one and split it into two, the pieces biting into a huge wooden cupboard, the knife into the back of a chair. My nostrils burned.

Poison.

Everyone else seemed to be moving in slow motion. Guards turned, eyes widening, fangs flashing. Swords gleamed, lace ribbons fluttered, and boots clomped into the wall as the best of them flipped out of the way of the other two stakes. A wire birdcage toppled, spilling the stubs of half-burned candles. Beeswax joined the sharp, sweet smell of the poison. One of the stakes caught a thin pale courtier in the shoulder when he failed to lean backward quickly enough. He yelled and even that sound seemed too slow and stretched out until it distorted. His blood splattered onto the tiles laid into the ground between the edges of the carpets.

The third stake went unerringly on its way, straight toward my mother's heart.

The girl smiled once, even as she fought to free herself from Quinn's grim hold.

Which just went to show how little she knew my mother.

My father whirled to put himself between her and the stake, as two of my other brothers, Marcus and Connor, somersaulted to his side to form a wider barrier.

Even as my mother leaped into the air and tumbled over their heads, refusing to use a shield made of her husband and sons.

She landed a little to the left and stuck out her arm, safely encased in a leather bracer, and knocked the stake right out of the air. It hit a tapestry and fell into a basket, looking innocuous. Guards closed in. There was so much snarling, the royal caves sounded more like cougar enclosures at the zoo. Mom fought her way free of her overeager guards as the girl was hauled away from Quinn.

"I want her alive!" Dad was shouting.

Too late.

The assassin-girl was clearly prepared, and knew enough not to be captured and questioned by the enemy. The inside of her vest was rigged with a slender hidden stake. She pulled a small piece of rope sewn into the armhole of her vest and smiled. There was a very small *thwack* sound and then she crumbled into ashes. Her clothes fell into a pile.

Dad swore, very loudly and very creatively.

Mom's fists clenched. "Quinn, Logan. With me. *Now*." She shot a glare at Marcus and Connor. "You too."

Mom did *not* like being saved by her children.

We followed her into a small private antechamber. Adrenaline was still coursing through me. Quinn's jaw was clenched so tightly he looked like a marble statue, pale and cold. I knew just how he felt.

We had a short reprieve as Dad cupped Mom's face and ran his hands down her neck, over her shoulders. "Helena, are you hurt?"

She waved that away. "I'm fine." She smiled briefly, then turned hard eyes on us. Each of us took a healthy step backward and not a single one of us felt any less manly for the wise retreat.

"I distinctly remember," she said softly, her long black braid swinging behind her as she crossed her arms over her chest, "after the events of last week, ordering you never to step between me and a weapon again."

"Mom," Quinn ground out. "Give me a break."

Her glare could have sizzled steak. "I will not have my sons killed by some third-rate assassin."

"And we won't have our mother killed by one either," I added.

She closed her eyes briefly. She looked less like an ancient Fury, pale as fire and just as angry, when she opened them again.

"Thank you, boys," she said finally. "I'm very proud of you. Don't ever do that again." She leaned against Dad. "You either, Liam."

"Shut up, dear," he said affectionately, kissing the top of her head. He looked at the guard standing in the doorway, under the string of small glass lanterns. The candles flickered. "Well?"

I recognized Sophie when she stepped forward. She had a mass of curly brown hair and scars on the side of her face from when she'd been human. No one knew how she'd gotten them. She bowed sharply. "The girl belonged to Montmartre. His insignia was stitched on the inside of her vest."

"And?"

"And that's all we know."

"That's not nearly enough," Helena snapped.

"I agree, Your Highness."

Helena sighed. "Don't 'Your Highness' me."

"Yes, Your Highness."

"Wait." Quinn frowned. "She had a tattoo."

"You're sure?" Mom asked. "Where?"

"Under her collarbone, above her left breast." To his credit, he didn't blush. Exactly.

Mom's eyes narrowed on his face. "You were looking down her shirt?"

Quinn swallowed. "No, ma'am."

"Mmm-hmmm. What was the tattoo?"

"A red rose with three daggers or stakes through it. I didn't get a very good look."

Dad frowned. "I don't know that insignia. I wonder if it's new?" He glanced at Sophie. "Find out. And double the patrols, and set another guard on my wife."

Sophie bowed and left the antechamber just as Mom started to bristle.

"Liam Drake, I can look after myself."

"Helena Drake, I love you, take the extra guard."

They glowered at each other. I knew Dad would win. Mom was vicious when cornered, but Dad had a way about him, like a snake hypnotizing his supper. His glower softened. "Please, love."

Her fangs lengthened with her annoyance. "Don't do that," she muttered, but we knew Dad would get his way. "Only until the coronation," she said finally, firmly.

Dad nodded. "Deal." He'd find some other argument come the coronation. The walkie-talkie on his belt burbled some garbled sentence. He pressed the button. "Repeat."

"You asked us to let you know when it was midnight."

Dad looked at his watch. "Right," he said to the rest of us. "The Hound delegation should be here any minute. Logan, you'll go meet them. If what we know about this Isabeau is true, she was turned just after the French Revolution. You'll be more familiar to her in that frock coat."

"Okay." I ignored my brothers' smirks out of long habit. They were strictly the jeans and T-shirt types. I couldn't help it if they had no style.

"The mountainside guards know to expect them, but no one else does," he added. "We didn't want the drama."

"All we get is drama." I rolled my eyes, leaving to make my way down to the main cave entrance. Dad's walkie-talkie warbled again. His voice went grim when he called out to me.

"Logan?"

"Yeah?"

"Run."

CHAPTER 2

Isabeau

I hadn't expected the ambush. And that's saying something.

I hadn't become a Hound princess in the year and a half since I'd been dug out of the ground because I was a trusting sort. If the French Revolution hadn't cured me of that, being bitten and abandoned by one of Montmartre's Host would have.

And I might have been taken by surprise, but I wasn't an idiot.

I was, however, armed to the teeth.

The guards outnumbered us. I'd only traveled with two others, Magda and Finn, since it was difficult to find a Hound who had the temper to deal with the vampire royal courts and the associated unrelenting arrogance. Magda's temperament was hardly stable, but she was beautiful and just, which mostly balanced everything else out. Finn was as serene as the cedar woods he loved so much.

And I was just me: lonely and vengeful but still as polite as the French lady I'd been raised to be. I was both eighteen years old and more than two hundred years old. As if this wasn't confusing enough, I'd been pulled out of the grave by a pack of witch's dogs.

Kala preferred *shamanka* to *witch*. Most of the princes and lordlings respected her and since she'd been the one to send me to the meeting, no one had argued or offered to take my place. I was her apprentice and that was enough for the others, even if I wasn't sure it was enough for me. I'd have been happier fading into the background, but I owed Kala my life, such as it was. She'd pulled me through the madness and made sure I didn't turn feral or fall prey to Montmartre. She claimed if I was strong enough to last two hundred years in a coffin, I was strong enough not to go savage too. I didn't remember the centuries in the cemetery, only brief images before I lost consciousness. But I definitely remembered the pain of being pulled out and reawakened. And it wasn't strength of character that had seen me through, or even Kala's considerable magic.

It was the need to find the Earl of Greyhaven and my thirst for revenge.

For the sake of outsiders, I'd been labeled a Hound "princess" even though we didn't have princesses or other royalty. It was a useful title though, since the new queen would be more apt to listen to me, even if they were probably expecting a savage girl with mud on her face who ate babies for dinner.

That was why Kala had sent me to the courts for the coronation of Helena Drake and her husband, Liam Drake; that and the fact that I and the other Hounds had kind of saved their daughter's life. Unfortunately Montmartre had gotten away, so I didn't consider the mission a complete success, even if everyone else seemed to.

I was here to represent the best of the Hounds, and I had a wolfhound puppy to present as a gift. Kala's wolfhounds were legendary; I had a full-grown one as a companion: Charlemagne.

And he was growling low in his throat, muscles bunched under his wiry gray fur.

"*La*," I murmured, pointing for him to stay behind me. I had no problem releasing him to attack, but only if I knew he wouldn't be hurt. And right now there was an arrow aimed at his throat.

"*Hounds.*" One of the guards sneered. I knew that half-disgusted, half-fearful tone intimately. We weren't exactly famous for our elegant table manners. It hardly mattered that half the rumors weren't true. We used them to our advantage. The more the others disdained us, the more they left us alone, which was all we really wanted in the first place. Let them worry about politics and hunters. We only wanted the caves and the quiet.

Well, most of us.

The puppy in the basket slung over my shoulder barked and I set him down. I drew the long slender sword strapped to my back, which the guards hadn't noticed yet. The moment I touched the hilt, both Magda and Finn sprung into action.

Learning to fight was no different than learning to waltz or dance the quadrille, in my opinion. It was all about the tension between you and your partner, about footwork and balance and timing.

And I preferred the long deadly sword to any silk ball gown I'd ever worn. I wasn't sure what that said about me, but I had bigger worries.

Like the polished mahogany stake flying through the air toward my heart.

I leaned back as far as I could. It passed over me, close enough that I could see the wood grain. Trust the damned royals to polish their stakes to a high gloss. We just sharpened sticks.

I popped back up again to crack my opponent on the side of the head with the hilt of my sword. I might have stabbed him into a pile of ash but Kala had warned us time and time again that we were here for negotiations.

Someone might try telling the guards that.

Magda took one out before I could stop her. It was hard to feel regret since he'd been about to snap her neck. Charlemagne whined with the need to jump into the fight.

"*Non*," I told him sharply. "We were invited!" I added, shouting as I cracked my boot into the guard's heel. He stumbled, dropping his stake.

"Stop!" Someone else hurled himself into the melee. Great, just what we needed.

He leaped between us, lace cuffs fluttering. He was pretty, like the boys I'd known at my uncle's parties, but not nearly as soft, even in his velvet frock coat. His fangs were extended, gleaming like opals. I didn't know who he was but the guards eased back, weapons raised respectfully even if they were still snarling.

"She killed Jonas," one of them spat.

"Because he was trying to kill me," Magda spat back unrepentantly.

The guard snarled. The boy turned to him, speaking blandly. "Don't you recognize them?" He pointed at me. "This girl saved your life not too long ago."

That hardly got the snarls to subside.

He looked about eighteen, same as Magda and me—though technically I was really 232 years old. Only Finn looked to be in his thirties, though he was nearly eight hundred years old. Kala had sent him to keep us level-headed. He wasn't really a Hound, just an ordinary vampire, but he'd been with us for so long that we treated him as if he was one of us, especially since he hated Montmartre as much as we did.

"My apologies," he added, bowing to us. "My mother's only been queen for a few days and everyone's still on high alert. Someone tried to assassinate her not ten minutes ago." He must be one of the legendary Drake brothers. There were seven of them and a single daughter who'd just been turned. "But you'll be safe," he hastened to assure us.

"I know." I did not need his protection. His eyes were as green as mine, like moss. I didn't like the way he was looking at me, as if I wore one of my old ball gowns instead of a leather tunic with chain mail over my heart.

"Isabeau," he said. "And Magda and Finn, I presume?" He nearly drawled each word. "I'm Logan Drake." His brown hair tumbled over his forehead, and the shape of his jaw and his narrow nose were distinctly aristocratic. He would have been more at home among the nobles of my time than this modern place. It made me both distrust him and feel oddly drawn to him. I straightened my spine. I wasn't here to admire pretty boys; I was here as Kala's emissary. It was inexcusable to be distracted, even for a moment.

"We're here for the coronation," I explained stiffly.

"It's not for another two weeks," another guard said.

Logan made a sound of frustration. "At ease, Jen," he said before offering us a charming smile. "If you'll follow me?"

I snapped my fingers and Charlemagne bounded forward to trot at my side. The basket full of wriggling puppy went over my shoulder again. They led us down a carved hall, the gray stone dipping low over our heads. Magda was scowling.

"These caves used to belong to us," she hissed.

"A hundred years ago," I hissed back. "You weren't even born then, never mind turned."

"So what? They still stole our home from us." Her long flowered skirt flowed around her ankles, the silver thread embroidery glinting in the torchlight.

"Lady Natasha stole the caves," Logan said, without turning to look at us.

"Are you planning on giving them back?" Magda snorted, before I could stop her. I pinched her arm. She jerked out of reach but didn't say anything else. Actually, she said a lot but she was grumbling, so we were able to pretend not to hear her.

The hall widened and finally brought us to a cavern dripping with stalagmites. Candles burned in silver candelabra and iron birdcages. There were numerous benches and a dais with the splintered remains of a white throne and dozens of cracked mirrors.

And vampires everywhere.

Conversations halted abruptly. They all turned to stare at us as if we were poisonous mushrooms suddenly growing in a manicured garden. They were pale and perfect, with gleaming teeth and hard eyes. I saw every manner of clothes, from leather to corsets to jeans. One of them wore a poncho such as Magda often wore. Finding comfort in the styles of one's human youth was common to all vampires. It was a similarity between us but it was hardly enough to outweigh the snarls and suspicious sneers.

Even Finn stiffened, and Magda was practically vibrating with the need to attack. Charlemagne's ears went back when he sensed the tension, thick and sticky as honey. Only Logan sauntered forward as if we were here for nothing more than tea and cake.

"I've brought our guests," he announced. No one could miss the inflection on the last word. And the warning. The conversations resumed, but mostly murmurs and whispers. No one wanted to miss the presentation between the queen and the Hound princess who helped save her daughter. I didn't see Solange anywhere. I put my shoulders back and swore to myself, yet again, that I wouldn't let Kala down.

Logan stopped in front of a slender, short woman with a long braid. I cast an envious glance at the daggers lined up neatly on her shoulder strap. The man next to her had wide shoulders and a calm smile.

"Mom, Dad, this is Isabeau St. Croix." Logan presented me with such a flourish, I nearly forgot myself and curtsied. He'd introduced me to them and not the other way around, subtly claiming that his parents had a higher social standing. I felt sure he'd done it on purpose but I was surprised someone born in this century would know those particular rules of etiquette. They hadn't survived the centuries, which meant I'd had to learn a whole new set of rules. As if it hadn't been tiresome enough the first time. "Isabeau, this is Queen Helena and King Liam Drake."

"Welcome," Liam said, his voice soothing and rich as brandy cream. I knew they were looking at my fangs. I had two sets, sharp and white as abalone shell. The more feral vampires went, the more fangs they grew. Even we avoided the *Hel-Blar*, who had a mouthful of razor teeth and blue-tinted skin. Before Montmartre, they had been rare. You could go your whole life without ever coming across one. They were mostly created by accident or ignorance, especially centuries ago when the bloodchange was even more of a mystery than it is today.

But now, because of Montmartre, they were like fire ants pouring out of an anthill; where there used to be one there was now a hundred. He'd been so eager to create his own personal army, he'd ravaged the old cobbled towns of Europe for hundreds of years, turning humans into vampires with indiscriminate greed.

That wasn't good enough for him though. He wanted his personal army to be the best, the strongest, and the most vicious.

He began leaving people half-turned under the earth to prove themselves, to survive the bloodchange alone. Those who didn't die, or go mad with hunger, were recruited to become part of his Host. The rest were abandoned as *Hel-Blar*.

And Hounds, or Cwn Mamau as we knew ourselves, didn't fit anywhere easily. We weren't regular vampires, we weren't *Hel-Blar*, and we most definitely weren't Host, as much as that fact irked Montmartre. We were a thorn in his side, seeking out the vampires he left underground and rehabilitating them before he could claim them for his own.

"A pleasure to meet you," I said politely. "Finn, Magda, may I present Helena and Liam Drake." Logan's mouth twitched slightly and I knew he'd caught what I'd done. Finn bowed slightly. Magda inclined her head stiffly. Her long brown hair and soft clothes made her look like a fairy princess but she was contrary by nature, and admitting to being nervous or inferior in a royal court, especially this one, was right out of the question. I laid the basket on the carpet and hoped our gift wouldn't relieve himself on the hand-embroidered roses. "I bring a gift from our shamanka, Kala."

Liam's smile was genuine when he bent down to help the puppy out of the basket. I watched Charlemagne carefully, who was studying Liam carefully. When Charlemagne didn't growl or tense, I relaxed as well. His instincts were sound. The puppy rolled over, barked, and then leaped to his feet, startled. Even Helena grinned. It softened her features considerably.

"Kala's witch dogs are legendary," she said.

"Yes, they are." I nodded proudly. I wasn't sure if she knew just how legendary they were. It was Kala's giant dogs that had scented me in the cemetery and dug me out with their claws. They'd been loyal to me ever since. And, truthfully, I preferred their company to those of my own kind. It was less complicated. "And Kala's not a witch, she's a shamanka."

"I beg your pardon. She says your gift for training them is just as legendary."

I tried not to blush; it was unseemly for a vampire. Still, Kala wasn't easy with her praises and I felt myself standing a little taller.

"You'll be our guest at the farmhouse." It wasn't a request. Even if it had been, there'd have been no polite way out of it. I wasn't sure which was worse, staying in these caves with those who clearly didn't want us here or staying in the house of the queen. She was making sure everyone knew we were under her protection but there was something else to it, I was sure. She didn't fully trust the Hounds, whatever her husband said about wanting treaties and reconciliation. This was a test.

"Of course." The amulets Kala had given me glinted in the soft light when I lifted my chin.

"Logan will take you there to rest. Your friends may remain here and acquaint themselves with the court."

Another test.

"Thank you." I ignored Magda's scowl; she'd been scowling since Kala first mentioned this visit. Finn bowed once and didn't say anything else, so I assumed he didn't have any serious objections. I wasn't yet used to the cavalier attitude to unchaperoned girls. True, I hadn't had a chaperone in Paris, but I'd been living in the alleyways pretending not to be a St. Croix. Anyway, we'd assumed they'd separate us; we'd have done the same if a group of royals or ancients had been invited to the caves. They might yet, if the treaties and negotiations went well. That gave me pause.

"I'll take you to the house." Logan smiled pleasantly at me. He didn't seem fazed by my extra set of fangs or the scars on my bare arms and the one on the left side of my throat. The few non-Hounds I'd met couldn't help but stare.

I hated being stared at.

I couldn't help but think Logan's eyes were knowing, as if he knew what I was thinking, when he motioned for me to precede him down the narrow cavern passageway curtained off with a tapestry of a moonlit forest. The embroidery was familiar. We'd hung similar tapestries in the château to keep out the drafts. Charlemagne padded softly by my side, alert but calm. I dug my fingers in his fur for strength when Logan wasn't looking.

"I take it from your accent that you're French?"

"*Oui.*" I didn't say anything else.

"Turn here. It's fastest," he explained, leading us down several more passageways and out into a clearing. He didn't pry but I could see the speculation in his quick glance. He'd ask more questions soon enough, he and his entire family. I tried to remind myself that I was Kala's emissary and strong enough to deal with the Drakes, royalty or not, ridiculously handsome or not. The moonlight glinted on the silver buttons of his frock coat. He really did look as if he belonged in a Victor Hugo novel, sipping claret wine by the fireside. "And this way we won't have to climb down the mountain."

The stars were thick overhead, visible only when the wind pushed at the cathedral ceiling of leaves and branches. The mountain was a black shadow hulking behind us. A wolf howled somewhere in the distance. Charlemagne threw back his head and opened his jaws to howl back. I snapped my fingers. "*Non.*" I was nowhere near comfortable enough to have him give our location away. I had no way of knowing who else walked the woods with us. I found it hard to believe they would send the queen's young son out with a savage princess without some kind of guard.

"The house is through the woods. We can take the tunnels if you'd prefer or . . ."

"Or what?"

"Can you keep up?" His grin was charming.

"*Mais oui.*" I was immediately on my guard. "I mean, of course."

"Great." He winked and then was gone. The leaves fluttered. Charlemagne whined once, excited. I felt the same way. I gave him the hand motion to release him and then we were both running through the woods, passing between huge oaks and maples, ducking under pine boughs, leaping over giant ferns. I'd never seen trees like these. I was used to the stately gardens and ancient vineyards of my childhood or, more recently, the Hounds' caves; not towering trees so tall I couldn't see their tops. Mists snaked at our ankles, drifted up to blow a cool breath around my waist. In the clear pockets, warm summer air pressed against me. My hair came loose of its pins and streamed behind me like a war banner. I would have laughed out loud if I hadn't been sure Logan would hear me and smirk. Somehow he'd known this would center me and calm me down again. I'd only been in the royal court for just under half an hour, scrutinized by barely a quarter of their numbers, and I was already itching for the seclusion of the caves and the uncomplicated company of Kala's wolfhounds. This was almost as good. I did laugh when Charlemagne charged through a river, splashing me unrepentantly.

Logan was still ahead. He was a blur and I was determined to catch up, if not pass him altogether. I knew his scent already, like the incense they used in church when I was a girl, underlaid with wine. Even under the thickness of the forest smells, of damp mud and decomposing vegetations and mushrooms, I could recognize it.

My boots barely touched the ground. A rabbit dove for safety into the bushes. His voice drifted back to me. "Come on, Mademoiselle St. Croix, nearly there."

I broke through a copse of thick evergreen and then I could see him, barely a yard ahead of me. I ran faster, feeling the burn in my legs, remembering how my heart might have pounded if I'd been able to move this fast as a human. We leaped out of the forest and into a field, landing at the same time in a puddle of mud hidden under a carpet of pine needles and wilted oak leaves. Only Charlemagne was smart enough to sail right over it.

Logan sighed. "These pants cost a fortune to dry clean." They were black, shiny like plastic or worn leather. These vampires worried about the strangest things.

The mud sucked at my boots when I stepped out onto the long grass. Barking erupted out of the farmhouse and I touched Charlemagne's head, whispering a command. His leg muscles quivered with the need to keep running, to meet the challenge, but he stayed by me. Logan shook his head.

"They weren't kidding when they said you had a way with dogs."

I shrugged. "We understand each other."

"He doesn't even have a collar."

"There's no need. He is not my servant, only my companion, and that is always his choice."

"Well, maybe he can teach our dogs some manners. Especially Mrs. Brown."

"Mrs. Brown?"

"Is a terror. And only about fifteen pounds of pug."

"Pug?" I echoed, interested despite myself. "I don't think I've ever seen one."

"Cross a small dog with a pig and you have a pug."

"Why would one do that?" I wondered.

"Lucy claims they're cute."

"Lucy is your . . . girlfriend?" Now why had I asked him that? I was suddenly too embarrassed to be proud that I'd remembered the modern English word for "girlfriend."

He slanted me a sidelong glance. "Lucy's my sister's best friend and pretty much like a second sister to me. She's the mouthy one, hard to miss."

"Oh."

"And you? Are you being married off to some Hound prince?"

"We don't have princes."

"But you have princesses?"

"Not really, but it is the nearest word to describe my position among my people."

"So will you marry for politics?"

I shook my head. "We rarely marry and never for politics. The bones lead us to our mates."

"The bones?"

"A ritual passed down through the centuries."

"And have the bones led you to anyone yet?"

"*Non.*" I had absolutely no intention of telling him the bones had told Kala I would find my mate in the royal courts. Or that she was rarely wrong in these matters. After all, her magic was so strong she had dreamwalked to find my tomb, projecting her spirit across the ocean to locate me with nothing more than an omen and a wisp of a dream. She could have ignored them to work her spells for some other, more personal purpose. Magic took as much as it gave, and one didn't just send one's spirit on such a far and dangerous journey without some cost.

So when Kala said my mate would be from the royal courts, she meant it.

And no Hound in the world would disbelieve her. It didn't bear thinking on. No other shamanka or shamanka's handmaiden had ever been joined with someone outside the tribe.

I'd rather be alone.

Besides, omens or not, I was here for another purpose.

"Hey, are you okay?" Logan reached out to touch my elbow, above a jagged scar from the mouth of one of the dogs that had pulled me out of my grave. I jerked back. He lifted an eyebrow.

"I am fine." I deliberately turned toward the farmhouse. The porch was wide with several chairs and a swing. Roses grew wild under the windows. The barking grew louder, punctuated with snarls. Logan looked concerned for the first time since he'd stopped a sword from cleaving my rib cage.

"The dogs have never met a Hound before," he said awkwardly. Even with my limited knowledge of him, I knew for a fact that he wasn't often awkward. It was endearing, more so than his charming smiles.

I climbed the stairs confidently. Dogs didn't hide their moods, didn't play games of manners or intrigue. Logan's hand was on the doorknob. "There's no need to worry," I assured him.

I felt better with three huge shaggy Bouviers charging at me. If Benoit were still alive, he'd have clicked his tongue at that. I didn't speak to the dogs, barely flicked them a glance. I just stood my ground and let them sniff me once before I snapped my fingers and pointed to the ground. Three furry backsides hit the marble floor.

Logan gaped at me. "Dude."

I gathered by his tone that he was impressed. When I was sure the Bouviers had accepted I was higher in the pack hierarchy, I let Charlemagne past me so they could meet.

The foyer was spacious, cluttered with boots and jackets and bags. The lamps and the overhead chandelier were lit. I tried not to stare. I was still half-awed by electricity. I might have woken up in the twenty-first century, but I still lived in a cave with amenities closer to the Middle Ages. I had recently allowed Magda to foist a cell phone on me but I still wasn't entirely sure how to work it properly. The first time it rang, I'd tried to stake it.

"Whoa." A girl interrupted my inspection. I assumed she was Lucy, as she was the only one with a heartbeat. I vaguely remembered her from the night Solange turned, staying close to her and trying to kick anyone who came too close. She'd hadn't been entirely successful, but she never gave up. "Did you give the dogs Hypnos or something?" she asked. She had brown hair cut to her chin and brown eyes behind dark glasses. She wore an excessive amount of silver and turquoise jewelry. There was a purse slung from her left shoulder to her right hip. It wasn't for a cell phone or lip gloss; rather it was stuffed full of stakes.

Two vampires followed her out of the living room; Solange, whom I'd last seen lying pale and dead in Montmartre's arms, and another one of her many brothers. They both stopped, watching me warily. It took Lucy a little longer. She glanced at them, then at me.

"What? What am I missing?" She sounded disgruntled. She tilted her head. "Hey, we know you. Isabel, right?"

"Isabeau," I corrected stiffly. I hated how polite and stilted I sounded. It was how I was raised but I knew enough to know it wasn't the way of modern people my age, vampire or not.

"Nice," she approved. "You don't look like an Isabel anyway. I'm Lucy, and that one's Nicholas. There's so many of them sometimes it's hard to keep track." She darted forward, arms out. I stumbled back, watching for a stake, knees bending into a fighting crouch. "Oh, sorry," she said. "I was just going to hug you for saving my best friend's life. I guess you're not the hugging type."

Logan sounded like he was choking back a laugh. Solange and Nicholas still hadn't said a word. Lucy turned to stare at them. "What is *wrong* with you two? She saved Solange's life." The irony that the human was more comfortable around me than the other vampires was not lost on me.

"I'm a Hound," I murmured.

Lucy shrugged. "You could sing boy band songs all day long and I wouldn't care." She shuddered. "You don't, do you?" That seemed to distress her more than the fact that the Hounds were rumored to be mad killers.

Logan rolled his eyes. "I don't think she's had a lot of exposure to boy bands, Lucy."

"But you do wear bone beads," she said, ignoring him and nodding at the beads hanging from the braids twisted at the nape of my hair. "Cool." She tilted her head. "You don't look crazy."

"You're like a runaway train," Logan groaned at her. "Can't you shut her up?" he asked his brother pleadingly.

"How?" Nicholas said somewhat helplessly.

"Kiss her, you idiot."

I happened to appreciate honesty, so it was impossible not to like her. She reminded me a little of Magda. "I guess you don't look crazy either," I told her.

Nicholas snorted. She jabbed him in the stomach with her elbow. "Be nice."

"You first." He rubbed his sternum. "Ouch."

Solange stepped forward. "I'm sorry," she said quietly. "You took me by surprise." She licked her lips. She still looked frail, for a vampire anyway. I wondered how she could resist the temptation of Lucy's heartbeat filling the house. "Thank you," she said. "I'm in your debt."

"We all are," Nicholas agreed.

"It's nothing." I looked away, embarrassed. "We have no love for Montmartre."

"Jerk," Lucy muttered. She stepped forward, breaking the uncomfortable silence by linking her arm through Solange's and then through mine, gingerly. Surprisingly, I let her. "Come on," she said cheerfully. "You guys can watch me eat chocolate."

The front door opened behind us.

"Solange, are you—"

He didn't finish his greeting.

Vampire hunter.

CHAPTER 3

Isabeau

I didn't think, I just reacted.

A Helios-Ra agent should not be able to breach the security of the Drake house now that they were the ruling family, especially when he had a broken arm. I might not consider them *my* ruling family particularly, but I wasn't about to let Solange get staked by a hunter after all the trouble we'd gone to to save her.

Shockingly, I was the only one who felt that way.

If I'd had a moment to let the group's reaction, or lack thereof, register, I might have wondered at it. They merely glanced at the intruder and were now positively aghast that I was flying through the air, double fangs bared.

I didn't like hunters.

This one was fast, I'd give him that. He slipped on the nose plugs that hung around his neck. It took him far less time to realize I was attacking than it had taken the others. The look of surprise on his face might have been comical if he hadn't been reaching for the release button on the Hypnos powder I knew was hidden in his sleeve. Once the secret was out about their new drug, it had spread like wildfire through the underground informants.

"No!" Solange yelled, but I wasn't sure whom she was shouting at.

I landed in front of the hunter before the Hypnos powder billowed in front of him, but only barely. I dropped into a crouch and rolled out of the way. I'd never actually experienced Hypnos, but I'd heard enough about it to want to avoid it. It had been created by the Helios-Ra as one more weapon in their arsenal in their fight against our kind.

Vampire pheromones could befuddle humans, could make them forget what they had seen or done, and could even make them succumb to us without the faintest threat of violence, if the vampire was strong enough. The Helios-Ra had grown tired of battles ending with their hunters wandering around perplexed and weaponless, or killed outright while they waited meekly for fang or knife. Certainly not all vampires were as civilized as the Drakes purported to be.

And now Hypnos was beginning to travel among the vampire tribes, making us vulnerable to one another in a way we had never been before. Pheromones didn't work on other vampires, but Hypnos, by all accounts, did.

I didn't have time to cover my nose and mouth. The powder

was so fine, like delicate confectioners' sugar on a poisoned pastry. I reached for a stake, fingers fumbling.

"Don't," the hunter snapped. "Don't move. Quiet."

I only took orders from Kala. I tried to leap to my feet but couldn't. The drug really was as nefarious as I'd heard. He had ordered me to stay where I was, and that was all I could do; I couldn't even move my mouth to speak. Even though every part of me screamed for release, every muscle ached with the pressure of it and my mind gibbered like a cornered badger, all teeth and claws and the need for violence.

But all I could do was lie there.

Charlemagne stood over me, growling, hackles raised. The Drake dogs growled in response but clearly hadn't yet decided who the enemy was.

Logan tried to approach me, moving slowly and warily. "Isabeau, don't panic."

Don't panic? *Don't panic?* I was virtually trapped inside my own body, unable to make it do what I wanted it to. I was at the mercy of royal vampires and a hunter.

I was an idiot.

I hadn't learned anything from Kala to protect myself in this situation mere hours after leaving the Hounds' caves. I probably deserved to die here in a puff of dust. But that would leave Greyhaven free, my first and second death utterly unavenged. Unacceptable. I actually growled, like the dogs, with my frantic need to be free.

"Isabeau, listen to me." Logan crouched to look at me since

Charlemagne wouldn't let him any closer. His eyes were very green, very intense. His jaw was tight. Behind him, Solange touched the hunter's arm, as if she worried for him. He took her hand in response.

This family made no sense.

"The effects will fade soon," Logan promised me soothingly, giving me his full attention. The light from the lamps made his cravat look like frozen snow. "You're not in any danger. I won't let anything happen to you."

I glared at him, then over his shoulder pointedly. He flicked his sister and her hunter a brief glance. "Kieran's a friend," he explained. "He won't hurt you either, I promise."

I wanted to tell him that I could look after myself.

But I couldn't.

I might never forgive any of them for seeing me this way.

"I'm sorry," Solange said to Kieran, then to me. "Really. He's not like the other Helios-Ra."

Kieran didn't look particularly flattered by that. He wore the unrelieved black of most hunters. He looked just like the other Helios-Ra to me. "Is she a Hound?" he asked, sounding stunned. His arm was encased in a soft cast.

"She's a guest," Logan snapped. Lucy crouched next to him, looking sympathetic. Charlemagne didn't move. A drop of his saliva hit my neck.

"I know it sucks, Isabeau," Lucy said. "Kieran did it to me two weeks ago."

"Shit," he muttered. "You guys had me tied to a chair."

Lucy waved her hand like that was hardly a good enough

excuse. "Whatever." She turned back to me. "You'll feel normal again in a few minutes. Promise." She really meant what she said, I could smell the truth of it on her even if I wasn't entirely convinced.

I couldn't stand the way they were all just staring at me. I knew what I must look like in my battle leathers and scars and double fangs and my angry dog by my side. I was proud of being Kala's handmaiden, of being a Hound, but the rest of the vampire tribes clearly didn't see us the same way.

"Let's give her some space," Logan said quietly, as if he knew what I was thinking. "I'll stay here. Why don't the rest of you wait in the living room."

"Are you sure?" Solange asked.

"I don't think she'll be too happy when she comes out of it," Kieran added doubtfully.

"Just go on," Logan nearly sighed.

When they left it was marginally less awful. I would have preferred to be completely alone. The thought of Logan seeing me at my weakest didn't thrill me. But still, there was a certain kind of comfort to his presence, which made no sense since we'd just met. Must be another effect of the Hypnos.

I tried to move again, but couldn't. I was able to speak though, which was a relief. It must be starting to fade. "Charlemagne," I croaked. "Ça va."

He sat on my foot, unconvinced but obedient. Logan stayed where he was.

"Do you want me to carry you upstairs to your room?" he asked.

"No," I said witheringly. I wasn't a delicate flower, I'd survived the Revolution and being buried for over two hundred years. I could handle ten more minutes lying on the floor. It had better not take longer than ten minutes. Though I couldn't remember exactly what it was like to lie in a coffin, I imagined it felt a little like this. I was glad I'd blocked it out, or lain comatose for centuries. Sweat gathered under my hair, cold on the back of my neck. It took a lot to make a vampire sweat. My expression must have been wild, because Logan cursed.

"This isn't how we meant to introduce you to our family. I hope you won't hold it against us for too long. The hunter is a little exuberant. He's not used to us yet either."

I snorted as control over my voice finally returned. "I can't believe a Helios-Ra hunter feels he can just walk through the front door."

"He and Solange have gotten . . . close."

"Does she have a death wish? We didn't save her to hand her over to the likes of them."

He shook his head, his tousled hair falling over his pale forehead. "He . . . loves her. Well, he's crushing on her anyway."

I didn't know the term but I understood its meaning well enough. I sighed. "I thought she'd be smarter."

He raised his eyebrows. "She's plenty smart." He looked thoughtful. "You don't believe in love then?"

"No." I wanted to look away, couldn't. "I don't know."

His smile was decidedly rakish. I'd seen its like on young aristocrats at my uncle's house. I tried to ignore it. I flexed my toes but wasn't able to do much more.

When the front door opened both Charlemagne and I tensed. I struggled to sit up, to reach for a weapon, any weapon. Logan rose and stood between me and the new arrivals. The four who burst in had to be his brothers, the physical similarities were too pronounced. Charlemagne growled, standing up again. They stopped mid-conversation, stared at the wild girl prostrate on the marbles.

I ground my teeth. This was hardly the way to foster respect for my tribe.

"Logan," one of them drawled. "Your technique's slipping if you need dogs to keep them from running away."

"Very funny, Quinn," Logan muttered. "This is Isabeau."

They froze each to a one, staring.

"Isabeau, my brothers: Quinn, Marcus, Connor, and Duncan. Sebastian's still at the caves."

"*Un plaisir*," I said dryly. My Hounds training might not have prepared me to be gracious under any circumstance, but my aristocratic upbringing had.

"Nice to meet you." Connor blinked. "Why are you on the floor?"

"Hypnos," I said.

Quinn snorted. "Dude, Hypnos and dogs? I thought you were the one who was supposed to be good with the girls, Darcy?" I recognized the nickname; I'd read voraciously once I'd grown accustomed to my new body and appetites. I'd needed to grow accustomed to hundreds of years of history as well.

"Shut up," Logan said. "Kieran blew Hypnos on her."

Quinn bared his fangs. "Why the hell did he do that?"

"Well, to be fair, she did try to kick him in the head."

Quinn grinned at me. "I like you already."

I tried to push myself up again. I couldn't lie there for another second while they stared at me curiously. I was too anxious to be able to retract my double fangs. If I'd been human, I would have been hyperventilating by now. Logan glanced at me, cursed.

"I'm taking you upstairs," he muttered. "Call off your dog," he added, scooping me up into his arms. Charlemagne was right there, pressed at Logan's knee.

"Ça va," I whispered, even if I wasn't sure I entirely believed it. Charlemagne trotted by our side as Logan climbed the stairs, carrying me lightly and easily. I was mortified and grateful. The conflicting emotions didn't make the present situation any easier to handle.

"I know you said you didn't want me to do this," he whispered. "But it's better than all my brothers cracking jokes over your head, right?"

I nodded because I didn't trust my voice. The fact that I could move my head enough to agree with him was heartening. He noticed the small movement.

"Any minute now," he promised.

The second floor of the house smelled even more like smoke and water. The far wall was faintly scorched. He followed my gaze.

"Hope," he said succinctly.

Hope had led a rogue unit of the Helios-Ra who'd kidnapped Solange and tried to burn down her parents' farm. It had only been a week ago at most and the damage was still visible.

Logan took me down a hall and kicked a door open to a guest room. The windows had thick wooden shutters with strong iron locks on the inside. There was a narrow writing desk and a padded chair by a fireplace. The mahogany bed was huge and soft-looking, with a small discreet fridge by the end table. I knew it would be stocked with blood. I was still young enough to need to feed immediately upon waking, something all the Drake children must also be dealing with. It raised my opinion of their hosting capabilities so far, drastically.

Logan laid me gently down on the bed, leaning so close that I could see the flecks of darker green in his irises. I swallowed.

"I feel like I know you," he murmured. "Is that weird?"

I didn't know what to say. Charlemagne hopped up to lie next to me on the quilt, breaking the moment before I could find a reply. Logan stepped back.

"I'll leave you alone," he said. "When Lucy came out of the Hypnos she broke Nicholas's nose. I'd wager you have a stronger swing and I happen to like my nose exactly where it is. No one will disturb you," he added fiercely. "Come down whenever you're ready. I'll be waiting."

He bowed. "*Mademoiselle.*"

The door shut very quietly behind him. When I could hear by his footsteps that he was down the stairs and out of earshot, I allowed myself a very small sigh. Charlemagne tilted his head curiously.

"This isn't going at all according to plan," I told him.

CHAPTER 4

Logan

My brothers are idiots.

Anyone can see that under the scars and the attitude, Isabeau is more fragile than she looks. And as a reclusive Hound princess, her first introduction to the royal family shouldn't be a dose of Hypnos and four idiots gawking at her.

If I'd managed not to gawk, they sure as hell could have. She was beautiful, fierce, and utterly unlike anyone I'd ever known.

It was really hard not to gawk.

Much better to pace outside her door with one of our Bouviers sitting at the top of the stairs watching me curiously.

"This sucks, Boudicca," I told her. "I don't think we inherited Dad's diplomacy."

She laid her chin on her paws. I could have sworn she rolled her eyes.

I hovered by Isabeau's door for another fifteen minutes until I started feeling like a stalker. Solange came down the hall from her room and met me at the staircase.

"She'll be fine, Logan."

"I know."

She tilted her head. "Did you change your shirt?"

"No."

"You totally did." She grinned. "Too bad your girlfriend tried to kill my boyfriend."

I snorted. "Too bad he dosed her with drugs. And she's not my girlfriend. I just met her. And lower your voice, would you?"

She raised an eyebrow. "I've never seen you like this."

"Shut up, princess." I mock-glowered at her. She narrowed her eyes at the term "princess."

"I will dye all your pirate shirts pink," she threatened.

I just grinned. "I'd still make them look good."

She paused on the landing, her expression turning serious. "Is it true an assassin tried to stake Mom?"

"Who told you that?"

She poked my shoulder. Hard.

"Ow," I said, rubbing the bruise. "What was that for?"

"For thinking I'm dumb and avoiding giving me an answer."

"I don't think you're dumb."

"Then stop trying to shield me, Logan."

"No."

She made a sound of frustration in the back of her throat.

I sighed. "Fine. Yes. Some girl tried to stake Mom. No one was hurt."

"Montmartre?"

"Yeah, she wore his insignia." I hated to admit it. Especially when her face went hard and her eyes flat. "But she staked herself before we could get any answers."

"Damn it." She slapped the wall, rattling the crystal chandelier above us. "He's trying to make me queen by killing Mom."

"Looks like," I admitted. I slung an arm over her shoulder. "But it's not going to happen."

She rubbed her arms as if she were cold. Vampires didn't really get cold, so it was more habit than necessity. "I hope you're right, Logan."

"I'm always right."

She chuckled, which is what I'd intended. "Careful, you'll be as vain as Quinn soon."

"No one's as vain as Quinn," Lucy said from the bottom of the stairs. She was carrying a mug of hot chocolate and a handful of cookies. Taking advantage of her stay with us, she was gorging herself on white sugar and junk food. She had more issues with her mom's tofu casserole than the fact that everyone currently around her drank blood.

"Where's everybody?" I asked. A fire popped in the hearth but the living room was empty. So was the kitchen.

"Fixing the wall outside," Lucy replied.

The north side of the farmhouse was a mess of scorched and water-damaged logs. The wraparound porch had taken the brunt of the attack when Hope busted out of the guest room and returned with the rest of her crazy rogue Helios-Ra agents. Bruno spent so much time in the home-improvement stores since then muttering his bewilderment at us on his cell phone that we'd started hearing "noises" in the woods so he'd stay home and patrol the perimeters. Hope had a lot to answer for. So did Montmartre. It really sucked that we hadn't gotten a chance to make them pay horribly and at great length. Defeating their plans didn't seem to be enough. A little vengeance might have been nice, regardless of what Dad said in his "rebuilding stronger" speeches. Truth be told, we were all just glad Solange had survived the bloodchange and the various attempts to abduct or kill her.

I was really glad not to be sixteen anymore.

Because being sixteen in our family just plain bites.

"I guess I should help them out," I said reluctantly. Manual labor was brutal on the wardrobe.

"Hell, yes, you should," Nicholas called out, emerging from the basement with an extra toolbox and a saw. Lucy grinned at him as he hauled the back door open.

"Tool belt," she said, licking hot chocolate off her lip. "Yum."

The wind shifted and I could smell the warm blood moving under her skin. We all could. Nicholas took a step back, looking vaguely pained.

She frowned at him. "What's the matter with you? You look nauseous."

"I'm fine," he said through his teeth. "Stay inside. It's not safe."

She rolled her eyes. "Quit fretting. It's perfectly safe, there's all of you and like a gazillion guards."

"That's not what I meant," he muttered, easing outside into the shadows to busy himself at a pile of cut logs. Tension made the tendons on the back of his neck strain. Lucy stared after him for a long moment before closing the door behind him.

I followed him, grabbing a stainless-steel thermos filled with blood from the cooler on the deck. I tossed it at him. He caught it and turned away to drink. It wasn't easy for a young vampire to resist the taste of fresh human blood. It was even more difficult when your new girlfriend was staying at your house while you struggled to tame the biting thirst. Now that Solange was newly turned, she had started to sit at the opposite end of the room and Lucy had been forced to move into one of the guest rooms, with a lock inside the door. We'd grown up with her and would never intentionally hurt her, but a young vampire was more animal than human in those waking moments after the sun went down. It was some sort of biological imperative. Our bodies forced us to drink what our brains would rebel against. Otherwise, we'd die.

"Hey, man, you're doing good," I told him quietly as he wiped his mouth with the back of his hand.

"She doesn't get it," he said. "Not really."

"She gets it more than anyone else ever could."

"Still."

"Yeah," I agreed. "Still."

Quinn, Connor, Marcus, and Duncan were ripping off the parts of the logs that were unsalvageable. I grabbed a hammer and tried not to be so aware of Isabeau inside the house.

Nicholas ran a hand through his hair, frustrated. "When did this all get so complicated?"

"Girls are always complicated," I told him. "You know that."

He half smiled. "Some more than others."

I thought of the scars on Isabeau's arms and the haunted look in her eye. "Got that right."

We got to work, mostly following Duncan's lead because he almost had a clue as to how to fix a wall. When we needed plaster for some reason I couldn't quite fathom, I went out to the garage to find some. On my way back, I paused, goose bumps suddenly lifting.

A noise in the woods.

Something quiet, subtle.

And unwelcome.

I couldn't alert my brothers without alerting whoever was lurking in the woods as well. I set down the bucket of plaster dust and doubled back toward the front door and woods on the other side of the lane. I peered into the shifting shadows of the rose-bushes and cedar trees. The faint moonlight glinted off the Jeep in the driveway. The lamps burned softly at the windows. I smelled roses, newly cut oak logs, blood, and lilies.

Lilies were never a good sign.

Montmartre smelled like lilies. And while I doubted he was loitering in the woods outside our farmhouse, I had no problem believing he'd sent minions to do his dirty work.

He was after Solange again, just as she'd said.

He wanted her to be queen, as the old prophecy claimed, and

more importantly, he wanted her to be *his* queen. He thought he could rule in her place, using her as a figurehead. And after tonight, he apparently thought if he took Mom out of the picture, Solange would fall in line.

He *so* didn't get Drake women.

And he really needed staking.

I was happy to oblige . . . if he would just stand still long enough.

CHAPTER 5

Isabeau

When the Hypnos powder finally wore off, it was quick as summer lightning, I reared up as if I'd been jolted full of electricity. Charlemagne barked once and I laughed out loud. The ability to control my limbs again was intoxicating. I felt as giddy as a debutante at her first ball. Even the cell phone vibrating in my pocket didn't bother me.

"Magda." I grinned into the receiver. No one else would be calling me.

"Isabeau? Is that you?" Magda demanded.

"Of course, who else would it be?" I stretched to make sure I could. Then I did a backflip somersault.

"Are you giggling?" she asked incredulously. "What did they do to you?"

"Hypnos."

There was a pause, a choked cough. "And that's funny why?"

"It's not," I assured her. "But it's just worn off."

"Are you in trouble? What are they doing to you? Don't they know you're a princess, or whatever? I'm getting Finn."

"No!" I stopped her before she could get going. "I'm fine. It was an accident."

"Are you *sure*?" she pressed suspiciously. "They're not like us, Isabeau."

"I know," I said. "Believe me. Even their humans are odd." Even though I hadn't met many humans since I'd been pulled out of the grave, I was fairly certain Lucy was unique.

"They have humans there?"

"A girl. And some guards."

"Did you taste her?"

"I don't think they'd like that." I could just picture the look on Nicholas's face.

"Is the Hypnos as bad as they say?"

"Yes." There wasn't a moment of hesitation. "Worse even."

"Bastards."

"Keep your voice down," I told her. "We're supposed to be here as diplomats, remember?"

Magda snorted. "I'm not the diplomatic sort."

I snorted back, feeling better. "I know." Before she'd accepted me as a sister, Magda had been jealous of my closeness with her mentor, Kala. She'd tried to cut off my hair in a fit of pique. After I'd broken her fingers, she'd immediately warmed to me and had been fiercely loyal ever since.

"How is it over there?" I asked.

"The Drakes are all right, so far," she grudgingly admitted. "But most of these courtiers don't want us here."

"Should I come back?" I wondered, concerned.

"As much as I'd prefer it if you were here, we're fine. We'll see you tomorrow. I'll eavesdrop as much as I can until then."

"Good." She was exceedingly skilled at it. "I'll do what I can here."

"Watch your back."

"You too."

I slipped the phone back into my pocket and then searched the room for traps, cracks in the wooden shutter that might let in the sunlight, anything out of the ordinary. I even sniffed the blood in the fridge but it smelled fine. They would have thought me paranoid, but Hounds were accustomed to looking after themselves. Between Montmartre and his Host and the disdain of the rest of the vampire community, we couldn't afford to let our guard down.

And I couldn't sit in this room much longer. I had work to do.

"Come on," I told Charlemagne, pushing open the door. "Let's go."

I had planned to go back downstairs but changed my course when I heard Lucy's human heartbeat from the other end of the hall, around the corner. I found her standing at the window with Solange.

"Isabeau." Solange searched my face with worried eyes. "Are you feeling better?"

I nodded. "Where's your hunter?"

She flinched. "He went home. We thought it would be best." Her eyes went from worried to warning. "He's under Drake protection."

"So am I, or so I've been led to understand."

"Of course you are," Lucy said, her nose pressed to the window. "Misunderstanding. No big deal."

Solange quirked a half smile. "You might try complete sentences, Lucy."

"Can't. Busy."

I was curious despite myself. "What are you doing?"

"Drooling," Solange explained fondly.

"I totally am," Lucy admitted, unrepentant. "Just look at them."

Lucy moved over to give me space. She was watching five of the seven Drake boys repairing the outside wall of the farmhouse, under our window. I had to admit they made an impressive picture, handsome and pale and shirtless, muscles gleaming in the moonlight. I couldn't help but look for Logan, but he was walking away.

Solange leaned back against the wall, bored. "Are you done yet?"

"Hell no," Lucy said. She'd left nose prints on the glass. Nicholas smirked up at her. She blushed. "Ooops. Busted."

"I told you they could hear your heartbeat," Solange said. "Even from up here."

"I can't help it. Even if they all know they're pretty and are insufferably arrogant," she added louder. "Can they hear that?"

"Yes."

"Good." She glanced at me. "Yummy, right?"

"I'm sure Isabeau would rather recover, not ogle my brothers," Solange said. "You remember how stressed you were after the Hypnos?"

"Please," Lucy scoffed. "This is totally soothing."

When Lucy finally let herself be dragged away from the window, we went down to the main parlor. One of the windows was boarded up and the smell of smoke was thick here as well. Lucy chattered away, which was a blessing. Solange seemed as reserved as I was, and without the cheerful human it would have been awkward and uncomfortable.

"Your tattoos are gorgeous," she said. "I'm desperate to get one but Mom's making me wait until I turn eighteen." She made a face. "They pick the weirdest things to be strict about. I mean Mom's got three and Dad has one. Doesn't exactly seem fair, does it?"

My sleeveless tunic dress bared my arms, which ran dark with tattoos. It hadn't been easy to get them to stay permanent. I'd had to get them all redone three times. Vampire healing tended to push the ink and charcoal out.

"I've never seen work like that," she continued. "You didn't just walk into a tattoo parlor, did you?"

"No, Kala did these with charcoal and a needle." Most of them had been drawn in the ritual that dedicated me to her service. The first one they'd done before I'd fully awakened, after the dogs found me. It was a greyhound circling my upper left arm, catching his tail in his mouth, surrounded with Celtic knot work. All the Hounds had one just like it.

"Ouch." Lucy winced at the thought of the slow tattoo process. Most of the others were also dogs chasing one another up my arms, accentuated with vines. "Still, they're totally cool."

"You're not afraid of me." It wasn't a question but a statement. She looked surprised that I'd mentioned it.

"No. Should I be? You saved Solange."

"Even vampires are nervous around the Cwn Mamau," I pointed out. I wasn't sure why I was insisting she be scared of me. I just hadn't had a lot of experience with unconditional acceptance, not from the revolutionaries in Paris and certainly not from other vampires. I felt the need to poke at the odd experience, like a sore tooth.

"Because you wear bones and do weird rituals in caves and paint mud on your faces?" she asked, grinning. "Please, my parents do that all the time. They're totally into shamanistic rituals and dancing naked under the full moon."

"Explains everything, doesn't it?" Solange glanced at me with a shy smile, inviting me into the moment.

"She is . . . unique," I agreed.

"She's also right here," Lucy grumbled good-naturedly. "And even with my wimpy human hearing, I can hear you."

It was all very surreal. If my life had taken a different turn I might have taken for granted sitting with girlfriends in fine silk dresses drinking tea and eating petits fours. As it was, I'd never done this before. I wondered what Magda was doing right now, if she was touring the caves or arguing with a guard. I'd wager arguing with a guard.

"Can I give you a word of advice?" Lucy asked.

"I suppose so."

"You have a great French accent. If a guy asks you to wear a French maid's costume, kick him in the shin."

"Especially if it's one of my brothers," Solange agreed.

Charlemagne started to growl. I frowned at him, looking quickly around the room for the source of his alarm. I couldn't find a thing until there was a thump at the front door. We ran for the foyer, Lucy considerably slower behind us. Solange looked through the peephole, then reached for the handle.

"Another gift," she sighed. "Honestly, I thought once the worst of the bloodchange pheromones faded they'd go away."

At the front stoop lay a package wrapped in red foil paper, white rose petals scattered around it. She reached down to pick it up but I grabbed her arm.

"Don't," I said. "It's Montmartre. I can smell him on it." I nudged her back, reaching for my sword. "Go inside."

I didn't wait to see if she'd listened, only kicked the door shut in her face. I was climbing off the porch when a pale shadow was suddenly at my elbow.

I only narrowly avoided decapitating Logan. He bent out of the way of my blade, graceful as a dancer. His pretty face was grim.

"There's someone in the woods," he said.

"I know. Host," I added. I knew that smell, however faint—blood, lilies, and wine. Montmartre's personal army always smelled the same.

"Stay here," he ordered.

"I'm a Hound," I told him. "This is what I do. *You* stay here."

"Like hell."

"Then stay out of my way."

"Like hell," he repeated.

We moved like smoke between the cedars and maple trees lining the drive, toward the fields bordering the forest. I kept my sword lowered so the moonlight wouldn't flash off the blade and give us away. Charlemagne padded beside me, eager but silent. The trees towered over us in their mossy dresses, branches crowned with leaves and owls and sleeping hawks. The ground was soft underfoot, ferns touching our legs as we passed. Even the insects fell silent; not a single cricket or grasshopper gave away its position. Only the river sang quietly to herself in the distance.

Logan stopped, jerked his head to the right. I followed his gaze, nodded once to tell him I saw what he saw.

A single white rose petal, trampled into the mud.

For someone who wore lace cuffs when he wasn't bare chested, Logan knew how to track. The wind shifted and my nostrils flared. The smell of bloody lilies was stronger now, thick as incense. We followed it, splitting up in unspoken agreement around a copse of oak trees. Logan went left, I stayed right. This, at least, was something I was comfortable with. Tracking the Host was what I did. It sat easier on my skin than polite conversation and royal politics. I was almost looking forward to it.

There were two of them left, though it smelled as if there'd been more. They were quick, but not quick enough. Logan went ahead to block them off and I crept in behind them. One of them hissed.

"Do you hear—"

He didn't finish his question. Instead he spun on one foot to face me with a leer. I didn't waste time leering back, only leaped forward with my sword flashing.

"A Hound whelp," he spat. "A little far from home, aren't you?"

"No farther than you."

He swung out with a fist, confident of his strength. I danced backward, cocked an eyebrow in his direction.

"Serving Montmartre's made you fat and lazy," I taunted him. His face mottled with rage and he roared, attacking again. Anger made him clumsy and easy to avoid. I flitted around him like a hummingbird. Charlemagne stood to the side, waiting for a command.

Logan engaged his companion before they could join forces. "Quit playing with him and finish him," he grunted, ducking a dagger strike.

The Host who was trying his best to dismember me had a similar dagger, curved and nearly as long as a sword. There was no crossbow, no gun loaded with bullets filled with holy water. It was a favorite among the Host, stolen from fallen Helios-Ra agents. This one, though, was dressed for hunting and infiltrating, not battle. I noticed these details dispassionately, concentrating on staying light on my feet. Our movements grew faster, more vicious until we must have looked like a blur, just a succession of colors, like paint smears on a wet canvas. Logan dispatched his opponent, ash settling on the nearby ferns. He bent to pick something up out of the clothes left behind.

I parried a stab at my heart, the chain-mail patch sewn into my tunic jingling faintly. I aimed for his head, moving with deliberate and deceptive slowness. He blocked it, leaning back instinctively. I took advantage of his position and the momentum of my swing and jabbed at his lower leg. I caught him by surprise and he stumbled back, cursing. Blood seeped down his leg, splattered into the undergrowth. I moved in for the kill but he was gone, running through the woods. I probably could have caught up to him, could certainly follow the trail of blood droplets.

Which was the point.

Logan wiped blood from a cut on his arm, shaking his head.

"You're as good as they say you are," he said. "I'm surprised you didn't dust him."

"Better to give him a few minutes' head start."

"Why's that? Didn't your mother teach you it's rude to play with your food?"

"I wouldn't drink from him if I was starving. He's wounded and he'll go back to his pack. If we're lucky that cut won't heal until he's led us there."

Logan stared at me, then at the thick green undergrowth. Even slowed down, the Host would be moving fast enough not to leave footsteps. Not flying exactly, but certainly a speed-enhanced float, which was difficult to track.

Much more difficult than tracking a trail of blood, even in a forest thick with the scents and markings of various vampires and assorted animals. Logan whistled through his teeth.

"I'm definitely impressed." He reached for the phone in his

pocket. "Let me make a call and then let's get the bastard. What the hell did they want this time? Solange has already turned."

"Montmartre," I said flatly. "They were leaving a gift for your sister at the front door."

"Son of a bitch. Is this a Host symbol?" He showed me the small wooden disk he'd plucked up out of the ashes of his attacker. It was engraved with a rose and three daggers. "The assassin who tried to dust my mother tonight had a tattoo like this."

"I've never seen it before," I said.

"There's something else going on here, something we're missing." He spoke curtly into the phone and then tossed his hair out of his eyes. "Let's go."

"I can do this alone," I assured him. "I'm quite capable."

"Mmm-hmmm," he murmured noncommittally.

We went swiftly, but not so swiftly that we'd catch up before he'd had a chance to lead us anywhere interesting. It was uncomplicated work.

The surprise came in the form of a piece of fabric, pinned to a narrow birch tree, gleaming pale as snow. The silk was indigo, faded with age and encrusted with silver-thread embroidery. The delicate stitching showed a fleur-de-lys and the frayed end of a tattered ribbon.

I knew that scrap of cloth, knew it intimately.

I shivered, reaching for my sword again.

CHAPTER 6

France, 1788

Her mother's dressing room was Isabeau's favorite place in the entire château. She loved it even better than the dog pens and the stables, even more than the locked pantry where the cook kept the precious blocks of chocolate and jars of candied violets. She wasn't allowed in either room, so she tried very hard to be quiet and unobtrusive, perched on a blue silk stool as her mother's maids flitted in and out with various cosmetics and gowns.

Her mother, Amandine, sat at her table, applying rouge to her powdered cheeks. Her hair was pinned under an elaborate white wig laden with corkscrew curls and bluebirds made out of beads and real feathers. Isabeau had heard stories of Marie Antoinette's beauty and the stunning displays of her hairpieces, some with ships so tall she had to duck through doorways. Isabeau couldn't imagine the queen could have been any more beautiful than her mother was tonight. When she was old enough, she would wear ropes of pearls and sapphires in her hair as well, and silk-covered panniers under her gowns.

Amandine's underclothes were made of the finest white linen and silk, ornamented with tiny satin bows. The gown she had chosen for tonight's ball was indigo, like a summer sky at twilight. The buttons were made of pearls and the silver-thread embroidery paraded fleur-de-lys from hem to neckline. The St. Croix annual ball was famous throughout the countryside; aristocrats traveled from as far away as Paris to attend. At ten years old, Isabeau was too young to join in but finally old enough to escape her nurse's attentions. She had already staked out a perfect hiding spot, inside a painted armoire with a cracked keyhole. She'd be able to see all the fine gowns and the diamond cravat pins and the pet poodles on gold-chain leashes. She bounced a little in her excitement. Her mother's glance slid toward her and she stilled instantly.

"You're very pretty, *Maman*," she flattered.

"Thank you, *chouette*." Amandine smiled at her in the mirror, clasping a necklace with three tiers of diamonds, pearls, and a sapphire the size of a robin's egg. She took a sip of red wine, dabbing her lips delicately with a handkerchief.

"I think you'll be even prettier than the queen. And our house is so much better than Versailles."

Amandine looked amused. "Do you think so, *chouette*?"

"Everyone says so," Isabeau assured her proudly. "They say the nobles pee in the back staircases, *Maman!* We would never pee on the floor."

Amandine laughed. "You are quite right, Isabeau."

"Except for Sabot," she felt obliged to admit. "But he's only a puppy."

Amandine's head maidservant plucked the gown off the hanger. "Madame."

Amandine stood up to let another maid tie her panniers into place and secure her corset. The gown slipped over the top. Isabeau scuttled forward to lift the hem so it wouldn't catch on the edge of the vanity table. It was surprisingly heavy and she wondered how her mother could stand so tall under all that weight. Her wig tipped precariously to the side and she caught it with one manicured hand.

"Francine," she said. "We'll need more pins."

"*Oui, madame.*"

When the wig was secure again, Amandine turned to admire herself in the long cheval glass.

"Oh, *Maman,*" Isabeau breathed. "*Tu es si belle!*" When she was grown-up, she was going to wear lip color and a heart-shaped patch on her cheek, just like her mother.

Amandine smiled. "I remember watching your grandmother prepare for balls." She reached for a hair-ribbon-length piece of cloth just like her dress. "Here, *petite.* I didn't need this after all. You may keep it."

Isabeau took it with a wide surprised smile. "*Merci.*" She rubbed it against her cheek reverently. She followed her mother out through her bedchamber down the mahogany steps, staying behind the maids. Her father, Jean-Paul St. Croix, waited at the bottom of the staircase. The duke was perfectly arranged, from his rolled wig to the gold buckles on his heeled shoes.

"*Ma chere*," he greeted Amandine. "Spectacular as always."

Isabeau kept close to the maids, sneaking behind a potted cypress tree when they abandoned her for other duties. She ran to the ballroom as fast as she could, ducking around footmen bearing jugs of wine and champagne, and servants carting gilded chairs and baskets of sugared fruit. She crept into the armoire, which usually stored excess table linens. Every single piece had been needed for the buffet tables at the back of the room and the more formal dining room across the hall, so the cupboard was empty. She fit perfectly inside once she'd drawn her knees up to her chest. She left the door open a sliver; it was even better than peering through the keyhole.

It didn't take long for the first guests to arrive. She could just imagine the beautiful carriages pulling up the limestone lane, drawn by magnificent horses with plumes in their manes. The footmen rushed through the ballroom, lighting the last of the candles and oil lamps. The crystal chandeliers glittered over tables laden with all manner of delicacies: strawberries, marzipan birds, sugared orange peels, roast goose, oysters, lavender biscuits, petits fours, and chocolate-glazed candies. Isabeau rubbed her stomach, which was growling at the sight of so many desserts. She'd missed her supper by hiding away from her nurse.

She forgot her hunger the very moment the guests began to

pour through the doors. The women laughed behind painted lace fans, the men bowed with sharp precision. She could smell the heavy perfume and eau de toilette mingling with the warm pâtés being circulated on silver platters. Champagne flowed like rivers at springtime. The orchestra began to play and the music filled every corner, even the dark space of the armoire. She imagined this was what angels' music must sound like, all pianoforte and harp and the soaring, ethereal voice of the opera singer.

Her parents joined the crowds just as the gaming tables began to fill up. Painted cards and coins changed hands. Someone's pet poodle growled at the singer. Isabeau felt her stomach clutch hungrily again and wondered if she dared escape her safe hiding spot. If she was caught not only would she be sent straight to bed, which would be mortifying enough, but she'd also never be able to use this armoire to hide in again. She chewed on her lower lip, considering. Finally the smell of all that food grew to be too heavy a temptation.

She eased the door open a few inches, waiting to see if she'd been noticed. A couple passed by, intertwined. They paused, kissing passionately. Isabeau made a disgusted face. The man looked as if he was trying to eat that lady's face. It didn't look comfortable at all. He should eat some supper if he was that hungry.

She slipped out, landing quietly to hide behind the woman's gown. Her panniers stuck out so far on either side of her, she was the width of three people. Neither she nor her companion noticed. They seemed to be breathing rather hard, as if they'd run a race around the garden. Isabeau abandoned them for the thick brocade curtains, pouncing from one window to another. Most of the guests were laughing too loudly, drinking strawberry-garnished champagne, and losing money with great shouts at the card tables. No one noticed her. It felt a little like being inside a kaleidoscope, swirling with colors and sounds and smells. It made her a little dizzy and she was glad for the relative safety of the buffet tables. She rolled under the first one she could reach, well hidden behind the floating white tablecloths.

From this angle, the gleaming parquet floor showed the scuff marks of fine shoes and beeswax drippings from the candles. She'd never seen so many silk slippers and silver buckles in her whole life. She couldn't wait to host parties of her own, just like this one.

She slipped her hand up the back of the table, where it was nearly against the wall, and took a blind handful. She'd been hoping for madeleines or a puff pastry filled with custard. The oyster was slimy and thick, though its shell was pretty enough. Perhaps she'd keep it on her desk and use it to display her treasures: a stone with a perfect hole through its center, a stalk of dried lavender, Sabot's baby canine.

The second handful was far more worth the risk of discovery. The cakes were light and smeared with icing and raspberries. They stained her fingertips red, like blood. She thought her teeth must be red too and she bared them like an animal, grinning. She'd have to remember this trick the next time she played with Joseph, one of the young stable boys. It would scare him silly and she would be avenged for the prank he'd played on her last month with that bucket of cold water.

She ate until she was full and sleepy and her teeth ached a little from all the sweets. She curled into a little ball and pillowed her cheek on her hands. One of the poodles sniffed his way toward her and lay down beside her, licking the last of the raspberry juice off her fingers. One by one, the little dogs found her, creeping under the tablecloth in their diamond collars to lick her face and snore themselves to sleep against her. Smiling, she fell asleep as well under her canine blanket, holding the ribbon of her mother's dress.

CHAPTER 7

Isabeau

The Host led us through the woods at a comfortable pace. He was stumbling enough to leave a trail of broken branches and blood. He healed quickly though and by the time he stopped in a shadowed clearing, there was only the scent of blood remaining, and only very faintly. Logan nodded to a tangle of blackberry bushes. The thorns would pull and scratch but it offered the best protection; everything else was delicate feathery ferns. We crouched silently, waiting. I tried not to remember how my mother had loved blackberry tarts best of all, tried not to feel the scrap of worn silk burning in my pocket. I was grinding my teeth loud enough that Logan nudged me, frowning.

I tethered myself firmly to the present, focused on the mud under our feet, the thicket of leaves, the white flowers glowing on the border of the meadow, the Host standing in the tall grass. The gleaming marble and gilded scrollwork of the château of my youth faded slowly. Dusty grapes became ripe blackberries, piano music became the silence of crickets sensing predators nearby, lavender fields became a dark forest.

The Host wasn't alone for long, as two more joined him from the direction of the Drake farms.

"They got Nigel," one of them spat. He was pale enough to gleam in the moonlight, as if he'd been covered in crushed pearls.

"Got me too," the one we'd tracked muttered. "Isabeau stabbed me, the bitch. Ripped my damn shirt. Since when do the royal courts have Hound whelps for backup?"

"Everything's changing, Jones." The third Host shrugged pragmatically. "Was Montmartre's gift delivered?"

"Doorstep," Jones confirmed. "As ordered."

Logan's lips lifted off his protruding fangs but he didn't make a sound. I was impressed at his control. I'd assumed the Drake brothers were a wild, undisciplined lot, being royal and all. It would have been easy to forget by their fine manners that they'd been exiled from the royal court since Solange was born, and strongly discouraged from attending for at least a century before that. They all carried themselves with a certain flair and confidence.

Jones was fully healed now and pacing a rut in the ground. "Any word from Greyhaven?"

The name hit me so hard I flinched as if I'd been struck, then I went as still as a hungry lion spotting a gazelle. A red haze covered my eyes, as if I looked through a mist of blood. If I'd had a heartbeat, it would have been loud as a blacksmith's hammer on his anvil. Time seemed to go backward, speed up, and then stop altogether.

"He's with Montmartre, waiting for the right time."

"We've waited long enough, haven't we?" Jones grumbled.

"He wants everything to be perfect this time. No surprises." The first smirked. "Well, not for us anyway. The Drakes will be plenty surprised."

I knew they were still talking but their words barely registered. All I could hear was that one word.

Greyhaven.

Greyhaven.

My skull felt like a church bell, ringing the same sound over and over again.

I hissed, tensing to leap out of the bushes, my vengeance closer than it had ever been before. They knew where Greyhaven was, could lead me to him so I could kill him for murdering me.

I never made it out of my crouch.

Logan was on me, quick as a hornet. His hand pressed over my mouth, his eyes flaring a warning above me. He was close enough that I could have bitten him, if he hadn't had my jaws locked together. His body chained mine to the ground. He was stronger than I'd given him credit for, but I was faster and could have flipped him into the nearest tree.

Only the realization that I'd been about to give us away altogether made me pause.

Even Charlemagne was smart enough to stay quiet, though he was trembling with the need to protect me. I wanted the fight with

Jones, with all of them, even if it meant giving away our only tactical advantage: a mere hint of a plan whispered by a group of Host in the woods. It wasn't much, but it was certainly more than we'd had at the beginning of the evening.

And I didn't care. I would have thrown it all away for a chance at Greyhaven.

And Logan knew it.

He stayed where he was, stretched out as if he were protecting me from a rain of fiery arrows, a crumbling mountain, some unseen danger. But the danger wasn't anywhere but inside my chest, circling like a vulture.

It took every ounce of strength I could muster not to hurl him off me. I forced my body to soften infinitesimally, molding me into the undergrowth. Even at that small surrender, Logan didn't move. His scent was strong: anise, wine, a faint trace of mint. I knew I smelled like scalded wine and sugar to him—Kala told me I always smelled that way when I was furious beyond logic. The rage boiling on my skin didn't faze him. His fangs didn't retract; his face stayed mere inches from mine. Most vampires cowered away from a shamanka's handmaiden when she was in this state. Logan was too busy listening to the others to cower.

"Any nibbles from the old guard?"

"Yes, most of those loyal to Lady Natasha's memory fled when the Drake woman murdered her, but a few stayed behind for a more subtle attack. They'll join with us when it's time."

"Good. Let's get the hell out of here. The Drake boys are probably still out looking for us."

The Host took off between the trees, toward the mountain. Logan stayed where he was and we stared at each other for a long, strange moment. In the shadows, his eyes were the color of sugared limes. Lovely and distracting, but not *that* distracting.

When our enemies were far enough away, I heaved him off me with a sudden violent jerk.

I rose into a crouch, panting. My body might not need air but breathing remained a habit, especially in times of stress. Logan hit the trunk of a birch and twisted in the air to land on the balls of his feet right front of me.

We both crouched, fangs bared, muscles tensed for attack.

We might have stayed there for the rest of the night if it wasn't for Charlemagne, who whined once, confused. It was like a flame was blown out.

Logan stood, all feral grace and ironic smile. He looked as comfortable and pretty as a guest at one of my parents' balls, even shirtless. I was still panting, nearly nauseous from the swirl of emotions swamping my stomach: anticipation, anger, regret, humiliation. My mother's dress, Greyhaven. It was very nearly too much. I stood slowly, like an old woman. Charlemagne pressed his cold nose into the palm of my hand for comfort and I wasn't sure which of us needed the comfort more.

"Are you okay?" Logan asked quietly.

I nodded jerkily. "I'm sorry." I was accustomed to being lauded for my focus and control.

"What happened? Do you know that Greyhaven guy?"

"*Oui.*"

His eyes narrowed on my face. "Who is he? What did he do to you?"

"What makes you think he did anything?" I stepped out of the blackberry thicket, scenting the air for any trace of Host. We were alone.

Logan's expression was grim. "Isabeau, I saw the look on your face."

I shrugged one shoulder. "I'm fine now. We should return."

I turned to walk back through the trees but he grabbed my arm. "You nearly lost it back there."

I stiffened. It didn't make it any more palatable that he was right. "But I didn't."

"Next time, you could put my sister in danger with your temper."

I swallowed a hot retort. "It won't happen again."

"I know," he sighed, letting his hand drop. For some indiscernible reason, I felt its absence. It was as if I were cold now, and I never got cold.

I didn't know what it was about Logan that flustered me like this. I was going to have to find a way to stay away from him. He clearly wasn't good for me.

"I can see it's not in your nature to give like that. Would you tell me what he did to you, anyway? Please?"

I lifted my chin, refusing to be pitied.

"He's the one who turned me and then left me in a coffin underground for two centuries."

We didn't speak again on our way back to the farmhouse. As far as diplomatic missions went, mine was already a disaster. I'd attacked a family friend, got doused with Hypnos, and nearly went mad with rage—all in one night.

No wonder I was so exhausted.

We'd barely been gone for half an hour, for all that it felt like days. Logan's brothers were all dressed and sitting in a grim half circle around the foil-wrapped package in the parlor. Solange was frowning at it, tapping her fingers on her knees. Lucy was asleep on the sofa, her head resting on Nicholas's leg. He'd draped an afghan over her, and she looked tiny and defenseless in a room of predators who couldn't help but hear the temptation of her heartbeat. She dozed on, utterly trusting.

"Did you get any of them?" Quinn snarled.

"Yeah, we tracked one, thanks to Isabeau," Logan replied wearily, dropping down to sit in a chair.

"And?"

"And we got minimal info and nothing we hadn't already guessed: traitors and surprise attacks."

"I can't believe the bastard got through our defenses." Quinn continued to seethe. He shot to his feet and prowled the room, his agitation rousing Lucy. She blinked blearily at him, then at Logan and me.

"You're back." She yawned. She glanced at Solange. "Quit staring at it so hard—you'll give yourself a migraine."

Solange pried her gaze away with visible effort, turning to me. "Is it safe to open it? I mean, Bruno scanned it and everything, so we know it's not a bomb or anthrax or whatever, but still. What do you think?"

"I would always rather know what I'm dealing with," I said.

Logan groaned. "You would so open the bomb every time, even when it's ticking right at you."

I wasn't entirely sure what he meant. I was still getting used to modern vernacular, and English at that, but Solange nodded fervently at me. "Exactly. These guys just want me to play Snow White singing in her little cottage while they do all the work."

Lucy snorted. "Snow White and the Seven Buttheads. You could give Disney a run for their money."

Nicholas poked her in the ribs. "I am not a singing dwarf!"

"No, you're a butthead. Weren't you paying attention?" She grinned and kissed him quickly.

"I'm opening it," Solange announced suddenly, grabbing the package.

Every single one of her brothers started to talk at once, voicing the same basic variation on two themes: "Don't" and "Let me." She ignored them and tore at the paper instead. The box underneath was plain white cardboard, the kind for transporting cakes. She bit her lip, pausing very briefly. Nicholas reached across to take it from her and she slapped his hand away without even looking at him. She lifted the lid, leaning backward slightly, as if she expected something to leap out of it like an evil jack-in-the-box. Her brothers did the opposite and all leaned in closer. Then we went as still as only vampires could go, prepared to attack, prepared for anything except what was actually in the box.

Lucy shuddered. "You guys are creeping me out. Quit it."

"That's it?" Solange asked, finally breaking the tableau. In the center of the box was a red velvet pillow displaying a small lump wrapped in red thread. It smelled strongly of rose water and cinnamon. My nose itched. "What is it?" she asked.

I knew exactly what it was.

"Isabeau?" Logan turned to look at me. I wondered what made him already so sensitive to my moods.

"It's a love spell," I said flatly.

"What?" Solange recoiled. "Ew. God. Do these things even work?"

"Sometimes."

Her eyes widened. "Seriously?" She stood up to put more distance between her and the box. "Why won't he just go away? I thought this would finally stop after my birthday."

"He doesn't stop, not ever," I said. As a Hound, I knew Montmartre and his Host better than anyone. "He has the patience of a snake and that's what makes him so dangerous, more so than his cruelty or strength or selfishness."

"Will he ever get it that I don't want to be queen and I sure as hell don't want to marry him?"

"No," I replied truthfully. "Not unless you tell him with the help of a stake through the heart."

She was pressing her back against the far wall; any farther and she'd be through the window and in the garden. "Um, is it my imagination, or do I feel funny?"

"It's possible." I stood up, sniffing at the charm. "It's very strong. Those are two apple seeds wrapped in red thread and a strand of your hair. He must have gotten it that night we stopped him in the caves. And that's a hummingbird heart it's all pierced into."

"What do we do?" The whites of her eyes were showing now, like a wild horse.

"Don't panic," Lucy said soothingly. "And what is it with you guys and disgusting hearts?"

"Lucy, I don't hate him right now! Not like I should!"

"I'll hate him enough for the two of us until we figure this out," she promised grimly.

"Let's burn it," Quinn said, reaching for the box and tossing it toward the dwindling fire in the hearth.

"No!" I cried out, leaping to catch it before it fell. The charm was pinned to the heart pillow, which I plucked out of the air. The box landed in the embers and caught almost instantly. Light flared into the room. Everyone stared at me. "Fire will only make it stronger," I explained. "Fire is passion."

"What about water?" Lucy asked. "My mom's always dunking stuff in water to purify it or cleanse it or whatever. She chants naked in the woods too."

Logan tilted his head, considering. I ignored him, grateful that vampires didn't blush easily. "No, not water either," I said coolly. "That would feed the emotion targeted by this spell: love."

Solange swallowed hard. "Can we do something fast? Please?"

"I need salt," I said, "two freezer bags, ice, and white thread."

Logan vanished and returned within moments with my supplies.

"Are you sure you know what to do?" Connor asked doubtfully. "Maybe we should ask around, do some more research? I could go online."

"I know what to do. This is what it means to be a Cwn Mamau handmaiden."

"I thought it was all about kicking Host ass."

"That too." I half smiled. "We are magic as much as we are aberration and genetic mutation." I dumped salt into both plastic freezer bags. "Surely, you've noticed as much?"

"I . . . guess."

I felt bad for them, to have so much knowledge and so little instinct. Magda had told me enough times that magic and prayer weren't relied upon in this century. It seemed a waste of tools to me. Anyone who had seen Kala work her magic would never think otherwise. I had nowhere near her experience but I knew I could handle a charm, even one bought by Montmartre. And there was no question he'd bought it off some witch—no one else would be able to make these bits of string and apple sing this way.

"Now what?" Logan asked.

The strand of Solange's hair was long, wrapped, and knotted in red thread. I worked it out carefully, tugging gently, patiently unwrapping even when Quinn came to stand behind me and scowl. Logan nudged him back a step.

I freed the hair and placed it between two ice cubes. I tied them into place with the white thread. "This will protect you," I murmured at Solange, concentrating on scenting the magic, as I'd been taught. I imagined the thread to be as impenetrable as a shield, as strong and sharp as a sword, as implacable as midwinter. "White represents protection and purification."

Solange nodded. "Okay. Use the whole spool, would you?"

Quinn growled. "Hurry."

I dropped the ice cubes in one of the bags and sealed it. I buried the apple seeds and the unraveled red thread and hummingbird heart in the salt of the second bag and added a layer of ice cubes to the top. I sealed that one as well.

"These need to be frozen."

Several hands stretched toward me. Solange was faster, though pale and tight around the mouth. "I'll do it," she said, her tone hard, brooking no argument.

She left and we could hear muttering and the slamming of the refrigerator door. Hard.

"In three days put them both in a jar of salt and sour wine and bury it at a crossroads," I advised her when she returned. "And don't let anyone see you do it."

"Can I spit on it?"

"By all means."

"Thank you, Isabeau. This is the second time you've stood between me and that horse's ass."

"*De rien.*" I yawned.

We hadn't noticed the dawn in our concentration. I'd been exhausted before working the charm; now I was beyond fatigue, though still pleased to have redeemed myself from my earlier mistake in the woods.

The others weren't faring any better, young enough not to be able to fight the lethargy that came with the sunrise. I felt weak as water, crumpling to lie on the carpet. Charlemagne curled at my head to protect my sleep. I saw Logan yawn as well and stretch out on the rug beside me. Nicholas was propped up on the couch, Connor slumped uncomfortably in a nearby chair. Only Marcus managed to crawl upstairs, but I had no idea if he'd made it to his bedroom. I was conscious just long enough to hear Lucy mutter.

"Vampires. Sure are the life of the party."

Chapter 8

Isabeau

I didn't know if other vampires had nightmares, but mine always came in that hazy place between dead sleep and sudden wakefulness.

It was the same dream every time.

It had been a full week since I'd last had it, the longest I'd gone yet. I'd never told anyone though I was pretty sure Kala suspected. She found me once, stuck in the loop of fear, wide-eyed and clammy, a crowd of dogs licking my face and trying to get me to move. Now it was strong enough to pull me out of sleep, even before twilight did.

Even though I didn't remember all that time trapped underground, the dream was always the same. I was inside the white satin-lined coffin, the fabric dirty and crawling with insects. Dirt crumbled through the cracks in the wood, and roots dangled like pale hair. I was wearing the silk gown I'd worn to my uncle's Christmas party but not the choker I'd made from the length of my mother's dress. That was as upsetting as being buried alive; I carried that indigo fleur-de-lys scrap with me everywhere, even in the alleys of Paris.

I scratched at the coffin and kicked my feet until my heels were bruised but I couldn't find my way out. I didn't even know if I was lying in a London cemetery or if I was in France. I couldn't smell anything but mud and rain, and the darkness that should have been complete seemed less than it was. I couldn't see clearly, of course, but I could catch the odd root, the pale white of parsnips, and the scuttle of blue-tinged beetles.

I screamed until I tasted blood in the back of my throat and still no one heard me.

And I wasn't hungry, not once.

The thirst, however, was maddening. It clawed at me like a burning desperate beast, raked across my throat, scorching all the way down into my belly. My veins felt withered in my arms. I was beyond weak, beyond alive, beyond dead. In a moment of clarity, I felt the wound of sharp teeth on my neck, felt a mouth suckling there until I was limp as a rag doll. And then the merest taste of blood smeared on my lips, which made me gag, or would have, if I'd had the strength. And it tasted like the wine Greyhaven had given me.

Greyhaven.

He let them bury me, even though he knew I'd had enough of his blood to taint me beyond any normal human death.

Greyhaven.

I wasn't strong enough to claw out of the earth, hadn't even realized it was what I was meant to do. It all seemed like some horrible accident, something out of a gothic novel. Earth filled my mouth, worms circled my wrists like bracelets, ants crawled through my hair.

Greyhaven.

And dogs howling, snuffling, digging with their claws.

That's when I woke up, every time.

The dogs were real enough; they'd been the ones who'd found me and pulled me out, even before Kala had pinpointed the right grave in Highgate Cemetery.

And Greyhaven's name was my first thought, was still my first thought when I reared out of that nightmare.

Charlemagne's nose lifted off my face when I stopped whimpering. I hated that sound, hated that it waited until I wasn't conscious enough to control it.

I was in a bed; someone must have moved us all out of the living room. The wooden shutters were bolted tight across the windows. I fell out of the bed and crawled to the fridge, yanking the door open. The light hurt my eyes and I groped blindly for a glass bottle filled with blood. The thirst was sharper in the evening, so sharp that I'd trained Charlemagne to defend himself against me if I spoke a certain word. The hunger wasn't easily leashed in our first nights. It still made me gulp the blood greedily, the way I'd eaten cake as a child, but I'd stopped actively worrying for Charlemagne's safety. This would be the same reason Lucy had grumbled earlier about being moved to a guest room with a double deadbolt lock on the inside and an alarm button connected to Bruno, the head of the Drake security detail. Newly turned vampires had little control over themselves upon waking.

When I'd drunk enough blood to have it gurgling in my belly, I straightened my leather tunic dress and left the relative safety of my bedroom. Solange and her brothers would sleep for another hour yet, so I made my way downstairs to let Charlemagne outside and check on the puppy.

"Isabeau."

I halted at the unfamiliar voice. A woman stood in silhouette against a tall arched window in the library overlooking the garden. Rosy sunlight fell into the room. I'd forgotten the glass in the house was specially treated; the wooden shutters in the bedrooms must be for added security and the comfort of concerned vampire guests. I certainly wouldn't have trusted a glass pane and lace curtains.

The woman turned, her face obscured behind a black veil attached to the velvet hat perched on her head. She wore an old-fashioned gown over a corset and fingerless lace gloves.

"Are you Hyacinth Drake?" I asked, courtesy pinning me in place. I'd heard Connor and Quinn talking about her. She was their aunt and had been injured by a Helios-Ra hunter. The holy water they used, charged with UV rays, had burned her face. It hadn't healed yet and no one was certain it would. Scars were rare on a vampire, but they were certainly possible. My bare arms were proof enough of that.

"Yes, I am. *Enchantee.*" She flicked a glance at the scars on my arms, then turned back to the window. That's when I realized she'd been watching Lucy running through the garden with the puppy, who was barking with hysterical glee. Lucy's laughter was nearly as loud. Charlemagne left eager nose prints on the glass door, then looked at me pathetically.

"Go on," I murmured, letting him out to join the melee. The puppy rolled over in the air in his excitement. Lucy laughed harder.

"Your scars don't bother you," she said. It wasn't a question, it was more of a flat statement. I shrugged.

"Not really." The half-moons and disjointed circles left by sharp teeth had faded to shiny pale skin, like mother-of-pearl. "I wear these proudly." I touched the puncture scars on my throat. "These I would burn off if I could." Since burning wouldn't help, Kala had tattooed that side of my neck with a fleur-de-lys.

"I was beautiful for so long," she murmured.

"Then you're still beautiful," I said bluntly.

"No pity from you, Isabeau," she said, and I could hear the faint smile in her voice. "I find that very refreshing."

"My people measure beauty by how quietly you can hunt," I explained. "And by how well you train a dog or how fast you run. We have tests to prove ourselves worthy and none of them have anything to do with the color of our hair or the shape of our nose."

"Then perhaps I should run away to live in the caves after all." Her tone changed, irony washing over the grief. "But I do so love my creature comforts."

Lucy was panting in the yard, wiping sweat off her face. The dogs raced around her like a merry-go-round. When she came toward the house, Hyacinth stepped back immediately.

"It was a pleasure meeting you," she said to me before disappearing into the depths of the house.

"Isabeau, you're up already," Lucy exclaimed, startled. The garden door shut behind her. She brought in the scents of summer rain, leaves, and fresh blood pumping under skin. I ground my back teeth together. "It's not even fully dark yet," she continued on heedlessly. The dogs milled at her feet.

"Sometimes, I wake early," I said. I had no intention of sharing my weaknesses and the violence of my nightmares. Like Hyacinth, I couldn't stomach pity.

Charlemagne blocked me suddenly at the sound of the front door opening and closing. I tensed. Lucy leaned back. "Wow, you're scary when you do that to your face."

"Get behind me."

"The other dogs aren't barking," she said quietly. "I don't think there's anything to worry about." A tattooed bald man in a leather vest marched into the room, jaw set grimly. I felt her stance soften immediately. "Bruno."

"Lassie." He met my eyes. "I want to talk to you."

"Bruno is the head of security," Lucy explained.

"But you're . . . human."

"Aye. Hunters like the daytime with most of the vamps lying around waiting to be staked. It evens up the fight." Though it was at odds with his expression, his Scottish accent put me at ease; the French and the Scots had often been allies. And I understood his bewildered frustration. His heart was practically pounding with aggravation. "We have the best security this side of presidents and kings, I want to know why in one bloody week a vampire faction and a Helios-Ra rogue unit have both managed to break through. It's bloody ridiculous."

"Montmartre doesn't care if his Host die. It's considered an honor, proof of loyalty," I told him. "I gather you would take it amiss if your people died."

"Yes."

"Montmartre just makes more Host. And last night they sent four with the purpose of only one making it to the front door. If they'd attacked outright, I don't know that they could have taken you by surprise."

He sighed. "You're right there, lassie. I was expecting a great deal of violence, not some ijit present." He shook his head. "Still, no excuses." He unrolled blue drawings of the farmhouse and the Drake thousand-acre compound with other assorted buildings. "Show me the weak point, would you?"

I went through the drawings, matching them with what I knew of the surrounding topography. "They would have moved from treetop to treetop. It's slower but stealthier."

"They came from above," he breathed out.

Bruno was smug by the time Solange and her brothers began to stir and trail downstairs.

"Are you ready?" Logan asked me. I nodded. Lucy scowled at Nicholas. He held up his hands defensively.

"Not my fault," he insisted. "Mom and Dad think you should stay out of the courts until after the coronation."

"That is so not fair," Lucy said. "It's not like I haven't already been there."

"Yeah, you were kidnapped by an evil vampire queen. Hello? Not exactly a point in your favor."

"When my parents come home next week I'm getting my dad to teach me how to ride his motorcycle and then I won't need a lift on your stinkin' bike anymore."

Nicholas grinned. "You think your dad's going to let you ride through the woods to hang out with a bunch of vampires in a cave?"

"He lets me hang out with *you*."

"Because I'm not the bad influence in this relationship."

She seemed to soften a little at the word "relationship." Then she immediately straightened her spine.

"I'm still annoyed," Lucy grumbled at him.

"You're cute too," he answered, unfazed. He leaned in and kissed her until she was nearly cross-eyed. Connor coughed.

"Dude, get a room."

Nicholas pulled away, grinning.

"Are they always like that?" I asked Logan as we left the farmhouse.

"You should have seen them before they decided they liked each other."

It was considerably easier to gain access to the royal courts this time around. The presence of five of the Drake brothers smoothed the way, even if it didn't completely erase the curious glances or suspicious, disgusted glares. It didn't bother me, but I noticed

Logan was glaring back at every single vampire who dared even to blink my way. It was kind of sweet, if unnecessary. He was close enough that his arm brushed mine.

"Isabeau!" Magda darted out from behind a cluster of bare birch trees in gold pots. She was wearing pink petticoats under an antique cream-colored skirt. She tucked her arm in mine, elbowing Logan away from me with a hiss. Magda did not share well. Logan didn't hiss back, he was too well brought up for that, but he did look as if he was considering it.

"Are you all right?" Magda asked, glaring at each of the brothers. Quinn smirked at her. She glowered more ferociously. "They didn't dose you with Hypnos again, did they?"

"No, of course not."

The courtiers drifted out of our way as we passed through the main hall, where they'd been hard at work. Since last night, the broken raven throne that belonged to the last queen had been carted out. There were fewer mirrors as well so that it didn't feel as if the crowd was twice its actual size. I felt better already.

"How was it here?" I asked her quietly.

"Fine, I guess. Finn is in his glory. He actually said three full sentences back to back."

I had to smile at that. Finn's long silences were legendary. "That's practically a monologue."

"I know." She scowled at a staring young vampire who didn't get out of her way fast enough. "I feel like we're some kind of circus show. Some guy asked to see my fangs. Can you believe that? And he asked me if we painted ourselves in mud."

Quinn chuckled from behind us. "That's called flirting."

She ignored him, even though it was bad form to ignore your host's children when on a diplomatic visit. It was worse form to attack their daughter's boyfriend, so I was in no position to criticize. I wondered yet again why Kala had sent me.

Everyone but Logan and Magda drifted away on their own errands. We went through several rooms, each more decadent than the last. One was decorated in red silk and velvet with gilded framed paintings on the wall. Logan made a face.

"Lady Natasha's tastes weren't exactly subtle," he said. "But we're keeping the paintings and we've started adding more. They're a lineage of ancient kings and queens and whatever."

There were dozens of portraits, framed and unframed, mostly oil but some watercolors and ink drawings. There were a few photographs near the end of the line. It was like being in a museum. I recognized some of the faces from legend and stories Kala had told us: the Amrita family, the Joiik family, Sebastian Cowan, who'd loved a hunter in the nineteenth century.

"That one's Veronique DuBois, our matriarch." Logan pointed to a small painting of a very dignified-looking woman in a medieval dress and wimple.

"Finn is drawing one of Kala," Magda added proudly, not to be outdone.

But I wasn't listening anymore.

On the end of the lowest row was an unframed oil painting of a familiar face. I knew the short black hair, the pale gray eyes, the smug smirk.

Philip Marshall, Earl of Greyhaven.

I took a step closer, feeling distant from everything except that face, as if I were underwater. The paint was still moist in one corner, gleaming wetly. This portrait had been done recently, hung before it was fully dried and cured.

I didn't know what to think of that. I felt my lips lift off my elongated fangs, felt a growl rumble in my chest. At first I thought it was Charlemagne. It took me a moment to realize the pained sound was coming from me. I curled my hands into fists, willed myself not to explode.

"Isabeau?" Logan stepped closer, concerned. "What is it?"

Magda insinuated herself between us, forcibly pushing Logan out of the way. "I'll take care of her," she told him darkly, putting a comforting hand on my shoulder.

"I'm fine," I murmured, barely recognizing my own voice. It was hoarse, but soft as water. I forced myself to turn my back on the wall of portraits, even though I felt Greyhaven's painted eyes boring into the back of my neck. I needed time to think. It was obvious to me, even without the warm tingle of the amulets around my throat, that something was going on.

"Let's go," I said, refusing to meet either of their gazes.

CHAPTER 9

Logan

I led Isabeau toward the antechamber my parents had reserved for private meetings. She seemed paler, her fingers tightening in her dog's gray fur, as if searching for comfort. I didn't think she even knew she was doing it. But I'd noticed. Something in that portrait gallery had spooked her. But I knew however many times I asked her, she wouldn't answer me.

So I'd bide my time.

For now it was enough to deal with the image of Solange making out with Kieran in a dark corner of the hall, where they thought no one could see them. Between Solange and her hunter and Nicholas kissing Lucy, Isabeau was going to think we did nothing but grope and flirt.

Which sounded just fine to me, but I didn't think she'd oblige.

"Dude," I snapped as Kieran's hand strayed under the hem of Solange's shirt. The cast on his arm was sharply white against his black clothes. The fact that he'd hurt that arm saving Solange was the only reason I wasn't currently yanking him right off her. "That's my sister."

Solange peered over Kieran's shoulder. "Go away, Logan. You're just jealous because you have no one to kiss. Hi, Isabeau."

I could kill her. She was just getting me back for the princess comment from the night before. And Isabeau would scare easier than a doe in hunting season if she thought for one second I wanted to feel her lips under mine. I narrowed my eyes warningly at Solange. "Shouldn't you be at the meeting?"

Kieran pulled away, having the grace to flush just a little. I didn't like the tempo of his heartbeat, or the direction his blood was flowing. "I have to wait for my friend Hunter," he said. "This is her first time in vampire territory and I promised I wouldn't go in without her."

Solange kissed him one more time just to annoy me, and then went to the antechamber.

"I begged Mom and Dad for a cat," I muttered at her back. She tossed me a grin over her shoulder, hearing me perfectly, as I'd intended. I grinned back.

"Helios-Ra really are allowed in the royal caves," Isabeau murmured as we trailed after Solange. She and Kieran gave each other a wide berth.

"It's crazy." Magda shook her head.

I shrugged one shoulder. "My parents want to do things differently. Dad's big on treaties."

"And your mother?" Isabeau inquired.

"She's big on making grown men cry," I replied dryly.

Isabeau's smile was brief and crooked and practically had me drooling. "I like her already," she said. She let go of Charlemagne. "I could use a moment," she said softly. "Are we expected right away?"

I glanced at the pocket watch hanging from my black jeans. "We have a good half hour. I just said that about the meeting to get Kieran off my sister's face."

"Are they betrothed?"

I nearly choked. "I sure as hell hope not. They've only known each other a couple of weeks."

"Ah." She and Magda exchanged a girly glance I had absolutely no desire to decipher. I decided to pretend I hadn't even seen it.

"Did you want a tour of the caves?" I asked, to distract us all.

"*Oui*. If it's not too much trouble."

"Not at all." I held out my arm, the way they do in period-piece movies. It would have been smooth too, if Magda hadn't glowered and shoved her way between us.

"I'm coming too."

I'd have to console myself with the hope that I'd seen Isabeau soften, even hesitate, as if she might actually have taken my arm. It was suddenly very easy to picture her in a gown with petticoats and ringlets in her hair and diamonds at her throat. It was just as easy to picture Magda with horns and a pitchfork.

"Let's double back to the main hall and start from there." I led them back, avoiding the portrait gallery. The hall bustled with activity, guards at every passageway. I took the one on the left, behind a tapestry of the Drake family insignia. Madame Veronique had sent it to us the night after Mom killed Lady Natasha. It was hand-embroidered and at least half a century old, with the royal mark of a ruby-encrusted crown along the top edge. Veronique had made it herself, long before Solange was even born. Apparently she paid more attention to vampire politics and prophecies than she'd have everyone believe.

"This tunnel winds around through most of the rooms," I told them as we ducked into the narrow stone walkway. It was lit with candles in red glass globes hanging from nails in the ceiling and it had a simple dirt floor and damp walls. Magda looked at me suspiciously but I ignored her. "All these doors we're passing lead to guest chambers." I nodded to an iron grate locked over a thick oak door with heavy hinges. "Blood supply's in there," I explained. "In case of a siege. It was Mom's first request."

"C'est bon," Isabeau approved. "We have something similar in our caves."

"There's a bunch of council rooms down that way, and a weapons store currently undergoing inventory."

"It's lovely," Isabeau said politely. "But where are your sacred stories, your paintings? Blood has magic, surely you know that much?"

"We have tapestries," I said, but I didn't think that was what she meant.

"Is it true your mother took out Lady Natasha single-handedly?" Magda interrupted, as if she couldn't help herself.

"Yes," I said proudly. "Sort of. None of it would have gone down the way it did if Isabeau hadn't arrived, just in time."

"So you admit you owe us?"

"Magda, hush," Isabeau said. "We all want to stop Montmartre. He's too powerful as it is."

"And a pain in the ass," I agreed grimly. "Not to mention a cradle-robbing pervert. He's what, four hundred years older than Solange?"

Isabeau glanced away. "I am technically two hundred years older than you."

"Not the same thing," I said quickly. "*At all.*"

Damn. If I tried, maybe I could shove my other foot in my gigantic mouth. So much for smooth. Magda grinned from ear to ear. I had no idea how to reclaim that lost territory. "I think we can all agree you're nothing like Montmartre."

Isabeau inclined her head, a glint of humor in her green eyes. "I do not want the crown," she agreed. "No Cwn Mamau does."

And the crown was pretty much all Montmartre wanted.

Aside from my little sister.

The thought made me grind my teeth hard enough that the noise startled Charlemagne. I relaxed my jaw through force of willpower alone. Then I realized I'd led us into a dead-end chamber. I'd been so distracted by Isabeau's scent and the sound of her voice and the way her black hair swallowed the flickering light of a single candle, that I'd practically walked us into a wall.

Hard to believe, but before Isabeau I'd had a fair bit of skill with the whole flirting thing.

She turned on her heel and I noticed she was smiling, a true startled smile, as if she wasn't used to it. "Oh, Logan, *c'est magnifique.*"

Apparently she liked cave walls and the clinging damp of mildew.

And then I realized her fingertips were hovering an inch over a faded red ocher painting. It was so faint I'd never have noticed it. As it was, I could only really make out a handprint.

"What is it?" I asked.

"It's a Cwn Mamau sacred story," she explained. "It's older than anything I've ever seen."

"From before the royals stole the caves from us," Magda felt the need to add.

"Hey, I've only been royal for just over a week." I felt the equal need to defend myself.

"Shhh," Isabeau murmured gently, as if we were bickering children. "This is a holy place. Can't you feel it?"

I felt the quality of the silence, the weight of stone pressing all around us. And if I concentrated, the very faint lingering traces of some kind of incense.

"This handprint here is the mark of an ancient shamanka. And here, these lines represent the thirteen full moons in a year." She pointed out the drawing in such a way that I could actually see it clearly, see the faint lines solidifying, see the dance of torchlight from centuries earlier, smell cut cedar branches under our feet. A slight wave of vertigo had me tensing. I must have made some sound as I peered around, because she smiled that crooked smile again. "You see it now, don't you?"

I nodded, turning to take in the cave drawings and the story they told. "Are you doing this?" I asked, stunned. "And *how?*"

"Simple enough for a handmaiden," she replied. "I just had to find the thread of this shamanka's story, the energy she left trapped in the painting." She pointed to the outline of a handprint done in spatters of red. "That's her mark."

"So I'm not insane?"

"No," Isabeau replied, just as Magda snorted, "Yes."

"Watch," Isabeau urged us.

A woman who I assumed was the shamanka shimmered into view. She looked about Solange's age, but with several long blond braids and symbols on her face and arms in mud and some kind of blue dye. She wore a long necklace that looked like it was made of bones, crystals, and dog claws.

She scooped red ocher paint out of a clay bowl and smeared it on the walls. There was chanting but I couldn't see anyone other than half a dozen giant shaggy dogs at her feet, and what looked like a wolf. Incense smoke billowed out of a cairn of white pebbles.

Everything sped up until the paintings were abruptly finished. There were dogs who looked as if they were breathing and moving ever so slightly, as if wind ruffled their fur. There were vampires with blood on their chins and a red moon overhead. There was a human heart, a jug of blood, a woman with a giant pregnant belly filled with squirming puppies.

"Cwn Mamau," Isabeau explained in a reverent whisper. "The Hounds of the Mother."

There was a religious feel to the artwork, simple and primitive as it was. The painted dogs lifted their throats all at once and let out a plaintive ululating howl that lifted the hairs on the back of my neck.

And then everything went dark, except for a jagged scar of red light near the edge of the low ceiling, in the back corner. The ocher dog painted underneath it growled.

Isabeau drew her sword from its scabbard. The holy feeling inside the cave shattered instantly. I reached for my dagger even though I had no idea where the danger was coming from. I tried to step in front of Isabeau to shield her. She kicked my Achilles heel and I cursed.

"You'll get yourself skewered on my sword," she said distractedly, still staring up at the red light. It was throbbing now, like a broken tooth. There was something decidedly menacing about it.

"Isabeau, be careful," Magda said tightly as Isabeau approached it. I stayed at her side despite the half hiss she threw my way.

"What the hell is it?" I asked.

"A warning," she replied, lowering her sword slowly. "When I tapped into the energy of this place, I broke some sort of cloaking spell."

"Cloaking spell?" I echoed. "That doesn't sound good."

"It's a standard charm," she said, shrugging one shoulder. "You can buy them off any witch or spellsinger."

"Witches and spellsingers," I muttered. "I keep forgetting I woke up in some sort of a fairy tale."

She shook her head. "Vampires who don't believe in magic," she said. "I'll never understand you."

"I didn't say I didn't believe in it," I replied. "Just that I wasn't expecting so much damn proof." I didn't even like the feel of the light on my face. I took a step back. "So what the hell was it cloaking?"

"A very good question."

She poked it with her sword, as if she didn't want to touch it either. Charlemagne growled once. There was a groaning sound and a pebble dislodged, then another and another. A broken boulder the size of a watermelon tumbled and hit the ground in a puff of dust. The weird red light went out, like a torch in a windstorm.

But not before flashing on a narrow, half-completed opening.

"Son of a bitch," I muttered, grabbing the candle and holding it inside. The tunnel was long and dark and freshly dug through the limestone.

"Someone is planning an unannounced visit," Isabeau said grimly.

"Montmartre," I bit out.

"He is quite determined," Isabeau agreed. "He will have many plans."

I hefted the boulder back up and shoved it back into the tunnel, closing it off again.

"What are you doing?" Magda asked.

"I don't want them knowing we found their secret passageway until we've decided what to do about it," I replied, rubbing my hands together to get rid of the dust. Frock coats don't come cheap and I'd already ruined one hurtling through the woods being chased by bounty hunters and rogue Helios-Ra on Solange's birthday.

"Oh," Magda said, sounding reluctantly impressed. "Good point."

"We should go back," I said, waiting at the regular entrance for them to pass through it. I didn't want them turning their backs on the secret tunnel, even knowing it was empty. "The tour is officially over."

CHAPTER 10

Isabeau

Helena, Liam, Finn, and two others I didn't know were waiting for us in an antechamber off a cave filled with bookshelves with glass doors to protect against the inevitable damp. An oil lamp burned on a table. Guards nodded at us when we passed through the doorway. I barely noticed. I was trying hard to retain my composure, to be the strong, dependable handmaiden Kala had trained me to be. This work was important, even if I didn't feel suited for it. Even if the nightmare from earlier was circling in my brain again like carrion crows over a fresh corpse. Not to mention trying to decipher the unexpected dreamwalk with the cave paintings. Truthfully, I hadn't expected it to work quite so well with a vampire as untrained as Logan.

Liam rose when we entered. "Isabeau," he said warmly. Helena lifted her head from the piles of papers and books in front of her. Finn nodded to me once.

"Liam," I greeted him, my voice carefully blank.

"I trust you slept well?"

"Yes, thank you."

"I apologize for the unfortunate event with the Hypnos," he added soberly.

"As do I."

"And I thank you for ridding our woods of Host and breaking the spell against our daughter."

"You're welcome."

"We owe you for that," Helena agreed. She shoved the books away. "Now can we please dispense with this courtesy dance and get down to it?"

Liam glanced down at her ruefully. "Love."

She shot him an equally rueful look. "Sorry." She turned to me. "I hope you're not offended, Isabeau."

"Not at all," I assured her. In fact, I was rather relieved to hear her say it. I was starting to wonder if that was part of reason I'd been chosen: not necessarily because of who I was but because of who Helena Drake was. Anyone else, Magda included, would have bristled and assumed she didn't think Hounds worthy of the usual protocol. I understood she was too direct to bother with political games. It made me suddenly hopeful about the alliance between our tribes. We were sick to death of games and politics.

"I'm rather envious of you, actually," she added.

I blinked. "I beg your pardon?"

"I'd have loved to have chased a Host down last night. Instead it was all treaties and protocols and hyperactive guards." She shook her head. "I'm going out hunting tonight, Liam, so you'd best get everyone to just deal with it."

She didn't seem like any mother I'd ever known. My own had been more interested in lace and dancing until dawn.

Logan grinned. "I don't think queens are supposed to hunt, Mom."

"Then I'll take Isabeau with me." She quirked a dry smile in my direction. "Then it won't be hunting, it will be alliance improvements."

"We'll make a politician out of you yet," Liam said.

"There's no need to be insulting." She sat back in her chair, her long black braid falling behind her.

"Mom, we found a secret tunnel," Logan told her grimly. "Very new, off behind the empty caves on the other side of the weapons room."

Her eyes narrowed dangerously. "Another one?"

He blinked at her. "There's more of them?"

"Two that we've found so far," she replied. "Your father won't let me fill them with dynamite."

"I'd rather not have the entire compound fall on our heads," he said dryly. "I'll take care of it." He spoke into his cell phone at a discreet murmur just as one of the guards opened the door. Suddenly the room seemed too small and constricting. Hart, the leader of the Helios-Ra, strolled in with Kieran and a girl with long blond hair. Her shoulders were tight, her hand hovering over a stake at her belt. She wore the black cargos and shirt that virtually every other agent wore while on assignment. I looked for the vial of Hypnos powder they strapped inside their sleeves but I couldn't find it.

"Hart," Liam greeted the other man with an amiable handshake. "Glad you could make it."

The blond girl and I were the only ones who looked as if we didn't think this was entirely normal. Well, and Magda, of course. She pressed closer to me, second set of fangs protruding slightly. Hart was handsome, dressed in a simple gray button-down shirt and jeans instead of camo gear. There was a scar on his throat.

"You know Kieran, of course," he said. "This is Hunter Wild." He motioned to the blond girl. "The Wilds have been part of the league since the eleventh century."

"How do you do?" Liam murmured calmly. "Have a seat."

Hunter nodded stiffly, eyes wide. Kieran cleared his throat, nudging her into a chair next to him. The rest of the Drake brothers filed in, stealing the last bit of air and space left in the room. Hunter stared at them. Out of everyone in the room, the vampire hunter was the one I could relate to most right now. My eyes would have bugged out of my head too, if I'd let them. This kind of group gathered together peacefully was unprecedented, outside of the old families on the Council.

"We can do good work," Liam said quietly. "If we let ourselves. We've called the Council. They'll be here in two days. Meanwhile, Hart has already agreed to work with us."

"What, and just give up killing vampires?" Magda asked. "And you believe him?"

Hart half smiled. "We're all learning a little discretion is all. We have a common enemy, after all."

"Montmartre?" I asked. I hadn't thought Helios-Ra was particularly interested in vampire politics.

He shook his head. "No, the *Hel-Blar*. Something has them running brave. We've never intercepted so many calls to the police about strange people wearing blue paint. I think we can agree they need to be hunted."

Magda nodded reluctantly. She had no love for the *Hel-Blar*; none of us did. It was too easy for the Hounds to remember that we might have been like them, but for a little luck and a little hidden inner fortitude.

"We've been getting disturbing reports all evening as well," Helena said. "The *Hel-Blar* are everywhere suddenly."

Magda hissed. "They're like cockroaches."

"Only rather more deadly," Finn agreed.

"Is Montmartre behind this?" Hunter asked. "I didn't think he could control them. Isn't that the whole reason for their existence?"

"We don't know," Helena replied darkly. "I'd really like to feed him his own—"

"Darling," Liam cut her off smoothly.

"Well, I would," she insisted. "*Hel-Blar* or not, he needs to be dealt with."

"Agreed."

"We can stop Montmartre," I told them confidently. "We nearly had him last week. He's not invulnerable."

"That's the nicest thing anyone's said to me all night," Helena told me. "But tell me the truth, Isabeau, would the Hounds ally themselves with us?"

"We all want to stop the *Hel-Blar*," I assured her. "And Montmartre."

"And after he's been stopped?"

"The Hounds will recognize no one but our shamanka as our rightful leader," I said delicately. "We will never be part of the courts."

Helena raised an eyebrow. "I've got enough vampires. I don't need any more."

"Actually, that's reassuring," Finn murmured. "You might try stressing that point as often as you can when it comes to the Hounds. They're rather keen on the right to govern themselves. I think you can understand that, given their history."

"We don't bow to Montmartre or anyone else," Magda agreed fervently.

"Do you think our tribes would be able to form an alliance?" Liam asked. "One that recognizes everyone's autonomy."

"I think so." Despite my natural misgivings toward the royal courts and non-Hounds in general, I genuinely liked the Drakes. I believed they were trustworthy, even if I had no actual proof of it. It was something I felt in my gut. "There are many superstitions and rituals that are dear to our people," I said. "Some Hounds will never agree to work with you because you've not been initiated, but they won't go against Kala either."

Hunter was staring at Magda and me so intently that Kieran elbowed her.

"Sorry," she muttered.

"She's never seen Hounds," Kieran told us.

"I can speak for myself," Hunter snapped at him.

"Well, you're being rude."

I glanced at him. "At least she didn't greet me with a face full of Hypnos powder."

Kieran went red.

Quinn grinned, lounging back in his chair. "She's got you there."

"Children," Helena said, half sharply, half fondly.

Hart's cell phone warbled discreetly. He glanced at the display. "I'm sorry, I have to take this. Hart here." His jaw tightened. "When?" He glanced at Liam. "Another *Hel-Blar* sighting. This one right on the edge of town."

Liam cursed.

"We've got a unit deployed," Hart assured him.

Liam nodded to Sebastian. "Take a guard and see if you can help." Sebastian was out the door without a word.

"I'll go as well." Finn pushed to his feet. "We may as well all start working together right away. Besides, we have a certain expertise in this matter that no one else has."

"But you're not a Hound, right?" Hunter pointed out, honestly confused. "You don't have the tattoos or anything."

"No, but I've lived with them for nearly four hundred years," he told her before following Sebastian. It felt odd not to go with him but I knew I was needed here more, however much I might prefer to run off and bash a few *Hel-Blar*.

"Let's reconvene in half an hour," Liam suggested to the rest of us. "We can compare notes and take it from there."

"Come on, Buffy," Quinn drawled at Hunter. "I'll give you the tour."

I took the opportunity to leave the small room. I was used to caves, dark and secluded, but ours weren't filled to the brim with people. Logan and Magda followed me, as if I had a plan. We were on our way outside when I paused, frowning. I touched my fingertips to the jumble of amulets at my throat. They were warm and vibrating slightly, as if they felt an earthquake no one else did.

"Something's wrong," I whispered.

Magda and I both reached for our phones, which rang at exactly the same moment. I didn't bother to answer mine. The chain of my amulet broke and scattered the pendants across the rugs. The wolfhound tooth capped in silver and painted with a blue dye made from the woad plant broke in half. I looked up to meet Magda's wild expression.

"Kala's hurt," she confirmed. "The Host attacked our caves." She hissed. If she'd been a cat, her fur would have lifted straight into the air.

I felt oddly numb. "I have to go," I told Logan, scooping up the amulets and stuffing them into my pockets. Charlemagne was at my side before I spoke the command. The courtiers whispered to one another as we rushed past them and out the other side of the decorated hall. "We'll be back for the coronation."

Logan grabbed his jacket from a coat tree. "I'm coming with you."

I didn't have time to argue with him and I was oddly comforted by the fact that he would come with me. Even if I didn't need him.

And I didn't.

"Tell my parents we're going to the Hounds. Their shamanka's been injured," he tossed out to one of the stern-faced guards at the entrance.

Magda and I were already scrambling down the cliffside, scattering pebbles. Something tumbled out of Logan's pocket when he caught up to us. He picked it up, bewildered. "What the hell is this gross thing?"

He was holding a gray dog's paw, the nails curled in. It was wrapped in black thread and thorny rose stems without blossoms. I went cold all over.

"That's a death charm," I said. "A rare Cwn Mamau spell," I elaborated when he just stared at me.

"It's a dog's paw," he said very clearly, dropping it into the dirt. "That's disgusting. I thought you guys liked dogs."

"It wasn't killed for its foot," I told him. "When our dogs die, of natural causes," I pointed out, "or in an attack, we use them for spell work, after the burial rites."

"Yeah, still gross," he muttered.

"And see this?" I pointed out a flat bone disk painted with a wolfhound and a blue fleur-de-lys. "That's my personal mark. Someone's trying to frame me."

CHAPTER 11

Paris, 1793

"*Papa*, I don't understand," Isabeau pleaded. "Why do I have to wear this horrid dress? It itches." The dress in question was gray wool without a stitch of ornamentation. She could pass for a maid-servant or a village girl. Even her hair was tied back in an uncomplicated twist without a single pearl pin or diamond bauble.

"*Chouette*, it's not safe anymore," Jean-Paul answered.

She'd never seen him like this before. Nothing scared him, not Versailles, not wolves howling in the woods, not even the huge spiders that crawled into the château just before winter fell. She'd seen him fight a duel once, when she was supposed to be asleep in her bed. Now he looked haggard and tired and nearly gray with grief. Her mother sat weeping in the corner. She hadn't stopped crying in days. Her hair was losing its curl, her face unpowdered. Isabeau shivered.

"This is about the king, isn't it?" she whispered.

He slanted her a glance. "What do you know, *chouette*?"

"That the mob took Bastille, that Paris is no longer safe."

"It's not just Paris anymore," he said quietly, shoving another wheel of cheese into the leather pack in front of him. They were in the kitchen, huddled by the hearth. Her old nursemaid Martine stood by the door, spine sword-straight. She wore a brown woolen dress and her hair was scraped back under a cloth bonnet. Isabeau had never seen her look so plain before. She shivered again.

"They've gained in strength and numbers. They've set up the guillotine as a permanent gallows. And the king was executed yesterday. France truly has no royalty now."

She stared at him, shocked. "They killed the king?"

"Do you know what this means, Isabeau?"

She shook her head mutely.

"It means none of us is safe." He wrapped a thick cloak around her shoulders. "Here, keep this on. It's cold outside."

She tied the ribbons together tightly. "Where are we going?"

"We're going to my brother's house in London."

"England?" she repeated. Her mother wept harder, choking on her sobs. "But you haven't spoken to him in years."

She was interrupted by the shattering of broken glass coming from the front of the château. She whirled toward the sound. Her mother leaped to her feet, her hand clasped over her trembling mouth. Her father tensed. "*Merde.*"

"There's no time." His eyes were determined, sharp as they found hers. "Isabeau, I need you to hide. Go with Martine, take your mother. You remember the broken stone I showed you?"

Isabeau nodded, her heart racing so fast it made her sick to her stomach.

"Pull it out and crawl inside. The passageway will take you out into the woods, by the lavender fields." More glass broke, and something hard thudded against the locked front door. She could hear shouting, faintly. "Do you understand, Isabeau?"

She forced herself to look at him. "*Oui, Papa.*" She understood perfectly well. She was sixteen years old and better equipped to protect them than her fragile mother.

"Then go! Go now!"

"*Non,*" Amandine shrieked, clutching his arm so tightly the fabric of his shirt tore under her frantic nails. The door splintered with such a loud sharp crack that it echoed throughout the château. Martine's face was wild as she grabbed Isabeau's shoulder.

"We have to go."

Footsteps crashed toward them. The mob shouted, knocked paintings off the wall, howled with hunger and frustration. The golden candlesticks in the hallway could have bought a winter's worth of food for an entire family. Never mind that there was scarcely any food to be had, bought or otherwise. January frost covered the fields and the orchards, and the summer crops had been thinner than usual due to weather and political upheaval.

Jean-Paul tried to tear Amandine's hand off him, to shove her toward Isabeau for safekeeping, but his wife was wild with terror and would not move. He wouldn't let her save him and he couldn't risk their daughter. They couldn't all get away, they'd be chased through the countryside, found.

"*Cherie*, please," he begged his wife. "Please, you have to go."

The mob was nearly on them. There was no time, no options left. He threw Martine a desperate glance. "Take Isabeau."

"*Papa, non!* We'll all go!" Isabeau struggled to convince him even as her mother fell completely apart in his arms.

Angry villagers poured into the kitchen in search of food, leaving a few others to vandalize and loot what they could.

"The duke!" a woman with gray hair shouted. She was so thin her ribs were visible beneath her threadbare chemise. Someone howled, more animal than human. The flames from a torch leaped to a tablecloth, catching instantly. The smell of burning fabric mixed with burning pine pitch.

Martine yanked Isabeau backward and out into the dark predawn kitchen garden before she could struggle. They landed in the basil, crushing the dried shrubs under them as they rolled to the shadows under the decorative stone wall.

"*Vien.*" Martine tugged on her hand. "*Je vous en prie.*"

"My parents," Isabeau said through the tears clogging her throat. "We have to help them."

"It's too late for them."

"*Non.*" But she could hear the shouting, the tearing of hands through the barrels of salted meats and baskets of dried apples. She could hear her mother's strange yelping, like a terrified cat, and her father's cursing as he struggled to shield her.

"Your father would never forgive either of us if we didn't get you to safety," Martine told her quietly, urgently. Isabeau knew she was right. Martine took advantage of her stunned pause to pull her off balance and drag her running into the edge of the woods. Torchlight gleamed from the kitchen window as more of the cloth caught fire. Smoke billowed out of the open door.

She watched her parents from the tall cradle of an oak tree. The mob dragged them to a farm cart and lashed them to the sides. Isabeau's father stared straight ahead, refusing to search for his daughter lest he give her away. Isabeau knew somehow that he could feel her there, up a tree, stuffing her fist in her mouth to keep from screaming out loud. Martine clung to the trunk beside her, her face wet with silent tears. The cart rolled away.

"I'll go to Paris," Isabeau swore. "And I'll find a way to save them."

Isabeau waited until Martine was asleep before making her escape. They'd found an abandoned shepherd's hut; the wooden slats were pulling apart under the wind and there was snow in the corners, but it was better than the exposed January night. They risked a tiny fire, barely enough to warm their toes in their sturdy boots. Isabeau drew her knees up to her chest and let her thick cloak fall around her like a tent. She closed her eyes and pretended to drift off until she heard Martine snoring softly. She was shivering lightly and the gray in her hair seemed more pronounced, the lines around her eyes deeper. Isabeau couldn't stand the thought of leaving her behind, but she couldn't expect her old nursemaid to go with her.

Paris was a death trap.

But there was no possible way she could go anywhere else. Her parents were being dragged there even now. They would be paraded through the streets, condemned of some royalist crime, and executed.

She had to stop it.

And Martine would have to try and stop her.

So it was best all around if she left now, before it was even harder. Her eyes felt gritty and swollen, her stomach was on fire with nerves, but underneath it all she knew she was doing the right thing. She left Martine most of the coins her father had sewn into her cloak, keeping only enough to see her to the city. Martine would need it more than she did. She'd have to find passage to England or Spain, or a villager to take her in. Perhaps someone would marry her. She was plump and pretty and dedicated; she deserved to be loved and taken care of the way she'd taken care of Isabeau her entire life. It should have been Isabeau's job to find her nursemaid a new position, a new family to live with; or else beg her parents to keep her on until she was married and had babies of her own. None of that was likely now. Marriage was the furthest thing from anyone's mind. The king was dead, Marie Antoinette was imprisoned, and most of the aristocracy had been murdered or fled to make cream sauces and pastries for the English.

Isabeau was sixteen years old, and she was clever and resourceful and she would do whatever needed to be done. She would free her parents and then find a ship to take them somewhere, anywhere.

She pushed the door open, wincing at the cold wind that snaked inside, fluttering the last of the fire. Martine moaned and shifted uncomfortably. Isabeau shut the door quickly and waited pressed against the other side, listening for the sound of Martine's voice.

Satisfied that her nursemaid hadn't woken up, Isabeau crept away from the hut. The night was especially dark without a moon to light her way. She was alone in the frosty silence with only a light dusting of snow for company. She walked as fast as her cold feet would let her, stumbling over twigs, keeping to the forest on the edge of the road.

She walked the entire night and didn't stop even when dawn leaked through the clouds. Her feet and her calves ached and she wasn't convinced she'd ever get the feeling back in the tip of her nose. She kept walking through the pain, through the cold wind and the growling emptiness in her belly. She hid in the bushes when she heard the sound of wagon wheels, not trusting anyone enough to beg a lift on the back of a cart. She might blend with her wool cloak and simple gray dress, but she knew her accent was too cultured, too obviously aristocratic, and that alone might make her a target.

The closer she got to Paris, the more clogged the road became, mostly with people fleeing to the countryside. Only radicals and adventurers and madmen went toward the city these days. She pulled her hood over her hair and lowered her eyes, keeping to the trees. Eventually they thinned to ragged bushes and then to fields and then she was on the outskirts of the city and everything was cobblestones and gray roofs in the winter sunlight. She'd been walking for three days with very little sleep and only frozen creek water to melt and drink. Her head swam and she felt as if she had a fever: everything was too bright or too dull, too sharp or too soft.

She stopped long enough to buy a meal and a cup of strong coffee to fortify herself. She huddled in her cloak, trying not to stare at everyone and everything. Smaller houses crowded together gave way to buildings, towering high and made of stone the color of butter. The river Seine meandered through the city, past the Tuileries, where the king had once lived, before they'd cut off his head. Isabeau shivered. She couldn't think of it right now. If she gave in to the grief and the fear she might never move again.

She forced herself to her feet and followed the river. The water churned under a thick, broken layer of ice. She rubbed her hands together to warm them, being careful not to catch anyone's eye. Men swaggered in groups drinking coffee and distributing pamphlets while women with cockades pinned to their bonnets stood on the corners talking. Their faces were serious, fired with purpose. Isabeau could smell smoke lingering and saw piles of burned garbage from riots and the fighting that took over the streets at night. She'd heard her father speak of it more and more, especially last autumn, when so many had been massacred.

She'd heard the guillotine had been set up in one of the city squares but she didn't know where it was. Her parents hadn't been to their Paris house since the Christmas she was eleven. She remembered passing the opera house in the carriage and the snow falling in the streets. She could walk in circles and never find her way.

She finally noticed that the crowds seemed to be heading in the same direction. She paused behind a group of women with chapped hands, smoking under an unlit streetlight. Taking her courage in both hands she approached them slowly.

"*Pardon, madame?*"

One of the women whipped her head around to glare. "*Citoyenne,*" she corrected darkly.

Isabeau swallowed. "*Pardon, citoyenne.* Could you tell me how to find La Place de la Concorde?"

The woman nodded. "Visiting *la louisette*, are you?" When Isabeau looked at her blankly she elaborated. "The guillotine."

"Oh. Um, yes."

"Not from here, are you?"

Isabeau backed away a step, wondering if she should dart into the safety of the maze of alleyways. "Yes, I am."

The woman shook her head, not unkindly. "Down this street and turn right."

"Thank you."

"If you hurry, you'll catch the last execution. Just follow the crowds and the noise. Robespierre got himself a fat duke and duchess." Her companions nodded smugly. One of them spat in the gutter.

Isabeau's stomach dropped like a stone. She broke into a run, dodging cafe tables and barking dogs and carts trundling slowly in the street. She could hear a loud cheer from several streets over, even with the pounding of her pulse in her ears. The cobblestones were slicked with ice and she slipped, crashing into a pillar of a large building. She pushed herself up, looking wildly about. All the buildings looked the same, stone and tall windows, pillars and pavement. She gagged on her frantic breath. Another cheer sounded, louder this time. She ran again, following.

She made it into the cacophony of the square just as the guillotine fell, the blade gleaming in the sun. There was a pause of silence and then more shouts. The ground seemed to shake with all the noise and stamping feet. The pressure of the noise made her nauseous. She'd never seen so many people in her life. There were guards with bayonets, hundreds of *citoyens* and *citoyennes*, children, urchins and pickpockets, and rouge-cheeked prostitutes.

Isabeau pushed through the crowd, heedless of the feet she stepped on or the bored curses flung her way. She struggled against the wall of people toward the dais in the center of the square. It was warm with so many bodies and the fires lit in braziers. At the very front, sitting in a row by the tall strange machine that was the guillotine were the *tricoteuses*, the women who sat and knit as the heads fell in the basket in front of them. If they sat too close, blood splattered them. They'd long ago figured out the exact perfect distance. Isabeau could hear their needles clicking as she pushed between them.

Just in time for the blade to drop a second time.

Her father's head rolled into a large basket, landing lip to lip with the decapitated head of her mother. Their long hair tangled together. Blood seeped through the wicker, stained the wood of the dais.

Isabeau's shrieks were drowned out by the enthusiastic spectators. She screamed herself hoarse and then felt herself falling and didn't even try to stop her head from cracking on the cold cobblestones.

CHAPTER 12

Logan

I wasn't about to let Isabeau go off without me.

I didn't care how long she'd known Magda, didn't even care that she was going back home to the tribe she loved. Her shield had cracked and I couldn't forget the glimpse I'd seen. And I hadn't been feeding her a cheap line when I'd told her I felt as if we already knew each other. Something in me recognized something in her.

But I wasn't stupid.

I knew she'd never admit to it—and not only because I was a Drake and royalty.

It still felt weird to think of myself as royalty. I was just one of many Drake boys with a handsome face and a smart mouth. I didn't stand out particularly; I didn't have Connor's knack for computers,

Quinn's right hook, or Marcus's gift for negotiation. I just dressed better.

"Can I assume you're not trying to kill me?" I asked as we ran on, leaving the dog's paw behind.

"I didn't make that charm," Isabeau said. "But I damn well want to know who's trying to muddy my name."

"And kill me," I reminded her dryly.

She looked remote and cool, but I could see the strain of worry under her polite mask. I'd never known anyone more self-contained than she was, running with her giant dog loping at her side, her sword strapped to her back. Magda sent me another glare, which I ignored. Someone materialized at my side.

"Jen, stay here," I told her. The last thing we needed was a hothead like her barging into Hound territory. She was armed to the teeth, stakes lining the leather strap that fit tight between her breasts, and there were daggers on her belt.

"Someone has to watch your back," she said stubbornly.

"I'll be fine," I insisted, annoyed. It wasn't like I was Solange with some deranged vampire lusting after me, or a little kid. I could take care of myself. I was eighteen years old, for Christ's sake.

"You're royalty," she told me, following me out into the dark forest. "I'm a royal guard."

I sighed irritably. I didn't have time to charm her or to shake her loose.

"Fine," I snapped. "But we'll be guests of the Hounds, so don't pick a fight."

"As long as they don't start anything, I won't either."

"I need your promise."

Her blue eyes sparked. "You have it."

"Less talking," Isabeau called back to us. "More running."

She was shooting through the woods like a star, her skin pale and glowing faintly when the moonlight found its way through the thick leaves. She had no idea how beautiful she looked, even grim and deadly as she was right now.

And I probably shouldn't be watching her ass quite so carefully but I couldn't help myself.

The forest went quiet at our approach. Five vampires moving quickly will silence even the cicadas. An owl rustled in a tree overhead but didn't fly away. I didn't know what to expect in the Hounds' caves. No one had set foot there uninvited in nearly a century even when they were backup caves and not the main residence. I'd been hearing stories about the savage Hounds since I was little. Isabeau had been a surprise to all of us. So had Finn, come to think of it, since he wasn't technically a Hound at all. He'd *chosen* to ally himself with them and they'd let him. I wasn't sure which part was more rare.

We stayed close to the mountain, skirting the huge pine trees. The wind was warm, even here. August was nearly finished, soon the leaves would change colors and fall away. It made it harder to stay undetected in the forest, but not impossible.

"Do you smell something?" Magda asked suddenly, slowing to a stop and frowning. She sniffed the air like a suspicious cat. Her expression went flat. "Blood."

My nostrils flared. Definitely blood. A lot of it. Despite

the situation, my stomach grumbled. My fangs extended instinctively.

"And something else," I added, hearing a soft tinkling sound, like ice in a glass. "Did anybody hear that?"

Isabeau nodded grimly. I shifted to be closer to her, even though Magda tried to block me. She acted like I was a threat, like I was planning to stake Isabeau when she wasn't looking. As if I ever would, and as if Isabeau couldn't stop me. I don't know what it said about me that it kind of turned me on that she could probably kick my ass if she wanted to. She might look like a porcelain doll, but I knew from experience that she was tough as iron nails. I'd have to find a nicer way of telling her that. I didn't think she was used to compliments. I may as well start getting her comfortable with it, because I planned to compliment her a lot. Just as soon as she stopped looking at me like she was trying to figure out what I really wanted.

Which was her. Just her.

I nearly groaned out loud. Having an aunt who'd slept with Byron and insisted we read all the Romantic poets had evidently addled my brain. My brothers would never let me live it down if they found out I'd fallen in love with a Hound princess after a single night without even kissing her. Like I had any intention of telling them. You didn't survive five older brothers and a younger one by running your mouth off about stuff like that. Basic survival skill.

We crept around a copse of stunted oaks and into a narrow clearing. It was the same one where we'd eavesdropped on the wounded Host after Solange received Montmartre's "gift." That couldn't be a coincidence. I saw the flicker of recognition on Isabeau's face.

But we didn't have time to discuss it.

At first, none of us knew what to say. I'd never seen anything like it. The smell of blood was so strong I actually had to cover my nose until I got used to it. The muscles in the back of my neck tensed up.

The long grass was undisturbed, dotted with wildflowers. The moon made everything silver, as if it were wet. There were no bodies, no drained humans or animals, no sign of struggle.

Just open uncorked bottles everywhere, dangling from string and wire from the branches. The sound I'd heard was the clinking of glass touching glass when the breeze rattled the macabre wind chimes. There were dozens of them.

"What the hell is this?" Jen muttered.

Every single one, from green wine bottles to jam jars, were filled to the rim with blood. Fresh, warm blood. All of our fangs were out now, Isabeau's double ones, even Finn's ancient opal-sharp ones. I took a step closer to a juice bottle, swallowing thickly. I could all but taste it. Jen's hand slapped my arm, forcing me back.

"Could be poisoned," she said.

She was right. We all froze. Isabeau turned a slow circle on her heel.

"It smells familiar, but it's not poisoned," she said finally, a kind of horrified awe in her French voice.

"It's not?" I echoed.

She shook her head. "It's a trap," she said. "Like a bowl of sugar water to draw the bees away from the kitchen."

I frowned. "A trap for who? Us?"

"*Oui.*" She reached for her sword just as Charlemagne growled in the back of his throat.

Hel-Blar.

They were everywhere. We would have smelled them if it hadn't been for the blood-saturated air around us. They had a very distinctive stench: rot and mildew and mushrooms. Their blue-tinted skin made them look bruised. Every single tooth in their mouth was a fang, sharpened to a needle's edge. And their bite was contagious.

And they were coming at us through the trees like spring rivers rushing into the same lake, like deadly blue beetles on fallen fruit.

Hell if I was going to be some ripe piece of apple waiting to be eaten.

"Shit." I reached for one of my daggers. I hadn't stopped to grab a sword, which was stupid. I'd thought a dagger and a handful of stakes would be enough.

Really stupid.

There was no sense in running since there wasn't a clear path out of the meadow. We could hear them growling and hissing, spitting like rabid animals. It made my jaw clench tight. The blood wasn't just tempting them the way it tempted us, it was driving them mad.

"Someone wanted them to attack us," I snapped at the others. "Someone knew we'd be coming this way."

"Host," Isabeau agreed in a voice like winter in the steppes. "Whoever attacked Kala must have set this up."

I leaped toward her, landing behind her to guard her back before the *Hel-Blar* reached us. She shot me a half-surprised, half-grateful glance. The moon glinted on her sword and the chain mail sewn into the leather of her tunic, over her heart.

"Stay close," I told her.

She snorted. "I have a sword and you have a butter knife. Staying close is about your only option."

And then there really wasn't any more time for witty banter.

The unnerving sound the air made as it sliced around them made me understand the old superstitions about vampires turning into bats. I bared my fangs. I had every intention of plucking them right out of the sky if I had to. The first wave hit hard, but at least half of their numbers were distracted by the bottles swinging over our heads. They drained them, gulping frantically as if they were frat boys at a kegger. Blood ran down their chins, dripped into the flowers. It was only a very brief moment though and then they all wanted the kill and wouldn't be deterred by bottles of cow blood.

The fight was fast and feral. We had skill on our side but we were outnumbered. And the *Hel-Blar* had battle frenzy down to an art. I killed one before he could get too close, but lost my stake in the long grass. He was too far for me to reclaim my weapon without leaving Isabeau unguarded. I had two more otaken.

"Shit, don't be a martyr," Jen yelled at me through her teeth. She tossed me one of her swords. She still had one in her hand and one at her hip.

"Thanks!" I caught it, grinning. I felt better already. I leaped over the thrust of a rusty rapier.

"Royal plums for the picking," one of them sneered. An empty bottle crunched under his boot. "Is this the way you decorate for your fancy parties?"

So they hadn't been sent after all, only lured and manipulated without their knowledge.

That was something to think about.

A stake grazed my left shoulder, leaving a raw burn in its wake. Later.

"Damn it, Logan," Isabeau shouted. "Pay attention. *Franche-ment*," she added in French. I could tell by the tone that it wasn't a lover's endearment.

She swung hard and blocked the attack of a screeching *Hel-Blar*. His arm, now unattached, sailed through the air and landed with a thud. It was still clutching a long stake soaked in poison. I could smell it, like salt and iron and rust. I kicked it aside.

Jen had dispatched two of them and Magda was shrieking back at one like a psychotic banshee. She might look like a flower fairy but she had wicked good aim. Dust puffed in front of her and she turned to the next one. Jen was nearby, hacking away with deadly arrogance in every swing.

A *Hel-Blar* thrust her dagger at me. I kicked out, snapping her wrist. The knife tumbled and she howled, then leaped at my head. We sprawled on the ground. A bottle snapped from its tether and landed by my head. Blood seeped into the ground. The *Hel-Blar* bared her fangs. They gleamed like needles. I cracked my elbow under her jaw and she nearly bit her tongue off. Saliva hit my neck. I fought harder until I managed to get my leg up enough to dislodge her. She hit the tree beside us and my stake dug into her papery heart before she could recover. She crumpled.

I leaped to my feet. Later, I'd feel bad I'd had to kill her. Right now, my mother's training was too strong, stronger even than the gentlemanly courtesies the rest of my family had instilled. I might wear frock coats and recite poetry better than sports stats but I knew the rules: you fought, you survived. And *Hel-Blar* took no prisoners.

Jen was proof of that.

I had time only to turn and the *Hel-Blar* she'd been fighting took her legs out from under her and buried the sharpened end of a staff in her chest.

"Son of a bitch," I yelled, using Jen's borrowed sword to cleave his head right off his shoulders. Then I stabbed him in the heart, pushing through his rib cage. But Jen was reduced to gray ash in a cup of primrose petals and clothes patterned with the Drake crest. I couldn't even stop to mourn her or hate myself for being the reason she was here in the first place.

Isabeau was tiring. I could see it in the arc of her sword arm, still deadly but infinitesimally slower. Magda was limping, holding herself up on a stolen broadsword, her hair matted with blood. We couldn't keep this up much longer.

"We have to get out of here," I said to Isabeau. "Now. Up into the trees maybe."

"Charlemagne can't fly," she said, and I knew that was the end of that half-formed plan. Isabeau would never leave her dog. She'd lie down and get staked first.

"Fine," I said, grabbing Jen's sword from under her empty clothes and surreptitiously slipping a bottle of blood into my shirt. "Then we do it another way." I stepped out of the safe ring Isabeau, Magda, and I had formed. Isabeau hissed at me.

"What are you doing?"

"Saving your very cute ass," I hissed back. Then I smirked my most arrogant smirk at the *Hel-Blar*. "Did you know royal blood tastes sweetest?" I dragged the blade across the inside of my forearm, biting back a curse. In the movies, no one ever mentioned how much cutting yourself open really freaking *hurt*. I held up my arm, blood dripping down to my elbow and spattering over the ground. Most of the *Hel-Blar* paused, turning to stare at me hungrily.

For this to be a rescue mission and not a suicide mission I was going to have to move *fast*.

"Come and get it," I shouted at them before throwing myself into the shadows between the trees, away from Isabeau and the mountain caves. I heard her litany of curses, all in French and all at the top of her lungs. Most of the *Hel-Blar* followed me, driven by bloodlust. They weren't stupid exactly, just mindless when it came to feeding. Only a few stayed behind to fight the others, which I felt certain they could handle.

I made sure my blood dripped everywhere, leaving a trail a blind puppy without a sense of smell could follow. Damn waste of blood, too. The *Hel-Blar* moved so fast I could barely hear their footsteps. I could hear them skittering though, like insects. They were really good at tracking.

So I'd just have to be better at escaping.

I pushed my legs as fast as they would go, until the forest blurred into smears of green and black on either side. The stench of rot hung heavy in the warm air. When I was sure they were well and truly distracted by my flight, I bent my arm and pressed the inside against my bicep to stop the flow of blood. The cut was already tingling warmly, which meant it was healing. I didn't want to leave a trail anymore though; it was time to get the hell out of here.

I slowed down slightly, in the interest of precision. I tossed the bottle aside, making sure it rolled in the undergrowth, spilling its bloody contents. Then I went in the opposite direction. I zigzagged a little until I was sure I was out of sight of any of my pursuers and then scrambled up an oak tree. I swung into the next tree and the next before finding a large enough branch to stand on with some confidence. I peered down into the shadowy green, searching for blue-tinted skin and needle teeth.

There were at least three *Hel-Blar* moving through the tall ferns. Acorns and twigs crunched under their feet. They weren't trying to be quiet anymore. Their teeth flashed. One of them stopped, sniffed the air in a surprisingly delicate way.

"He's here."

I tightened my grip on my sword and shifted slightly. I could probably leap down and land right on his head if I timed it right.

Instead, he gurgled and turned to ash. A stake dropped into

the grass where he'd been standing. His companion whirled and also crumpled. Isabeau pushed through the bushes, stopped under my tree. She looked up at me, her face unreadable.

"Don't do that again."

CHAPTER 13

Logan

I'd never seen so many dogs in my entire life.

Even though I hadn't known what to expect, this still wasn't it.

There were several cave entrances, the main one guarded by two Hounds with Rottweilers. The Rottweilers were happier to see me than the Hounds. They hissed at me but they bowed their heads to Isabeau with respect.

Inside was a wide opening leading to the back and several more doorways carved into the rock on either side. Some of these were barred with black iron gates, the kind you find in old wine caves in Europe.

"Private homes," Isabeau explained, her tone clipped. Her brow was furrowed with worry. She hurried down the main hall, down a few steps and then out onto a narrow rock ledge.

It was beautiful.

Everyone spoke of the reclusive Hounds as if they lived in holes and burrows in the ground, like badgers. But this main cavern was straight out of a Lord of the Rings movie set and it fit the name they called themselves, Cwn Mamau. Lit torches and fires kept the damp away and caught the amethyst and quartz imbedded in the walls, flickering like lightning bugs in a jar. Red ocher paintings of dogs and people with antlers and raised hands leaped in the torchlight. On our right, a waterfall fell like glass down into a pool of milky blue water. There were at least two dozen dogs, who all lifted their heads at our approach. We took the uneven stairs, which carved into a meandering trail. Isabeau practically leaped the last few steps, running to a woman lying on a bed of furs by the underground pond.

"Kala," she cried.

Kala was the infamous Hound shamanka who was rumored to have witch dogs and magical powers. She was also the closest thing Isabeau had to a queen, or a mother. Possibly both. The old woman had long white hair twisted into braids and dreadlocks and hung with beads made of bone carved into roses and skulls. She had blue tattoos in bold spiral patterns reaching from her left temple all the way down her arm and across her collarbone. Her eyes were so pale they were nearly colorless. There was blood on her teeth when she smiled.

"Isabeau."

Hounds floated toward us out of the fissures and nooks like moths converging on a flame. I kept my hand on my borrowed sword, but I didn't unsheathe it. I tried one of my most charming smiles.

Nothing.

I shifted so I wouldn't knock Isabeau off her feet if I needed to fight.

"Is this your young man?" Kala whispered hoarsely. Isabeau flicked me a glance.

"This is Logan Drake," she said. "Logan, this is Kala."

"Nice to meet you." My training was such that I could bow and keep a grip on my weapon at the same time.

Kala cackled. There was no other word for it.

"Told you the bones never lie," she said. I could have sworn Isabeau blushed. Magda looked at her sharply, then at me.

"What?" I asked.

"This is hardly the time," Isabeau murmured. "And it's not like that."

I didn't know what she was talking about but I very much doubted I would agree with her.

Isabeau smoothed a braid off Kala's cheek. "Where are you hurt? What's been done?"

Kala patted her arm. "I'll be fine. I've had blood and my ankle has already reset itself. You didn't have to come back."

"Yes, I did," Isabeau replied fiercely. "Who did this to you? Host?"

She sighed. "Yes. I went out to gather more mushrooms for the sacred tea and they ambushed me."

If she needed mushroom tea, I nearly said, she could have

bought some from anyone wandering the alleys in Violet Hill at night, and some of the farmsteads as well. Violet Hill was nothing if not a progressive hippie town.

"Did you go alone?" Isabeau frowned. "You know you should take someone with you. Kala, you're no good in a fight."

I was surprised to hear that. I'd assume the leader of such a ferocious tribe would be deadly with every weapon imaginable.

"Just because I'm a vampire doesn't mean I'm a warrior," Kala said to me. She clearly had other talents, like mind reading.

"Did you recognize any of them?" Magda asked.

Kala tried to sit up, settling instead against the back of a huge black dog of indeterminate breed. "No, there were a few of them. Their auras were strange and it distracted me. Dogs ran them off before I could get a good look. Hello, old boy," she added when Charlemagne licked the side of her face. "They could have staked me. They chose not to."

Isabeau sat back on her heels. "*Merde.*" She met my eyes grimly. I had to fight the urge to put my hand on her shoulder for comfort. She'd probably break my arm if I tried. Damned if that didn't make me like her even more. I was totally screwed. "If they didn't want to kill Kala, then they meant to create a distraction."

"And to get us out of the royal caves and in the path of that *Hel-Blar* trap."

"I don't like being yanked about like a marionette," Isabeau said darkly.

"I didn't think you would," I said dryly.

She rose to her feet. "Are you sure you're all right?" Isabeau asked Kala.

Kala nodded. "I'll be fine."

"Then I have to go and think," she said, mostly to herself, before stalking off, Charlemagne at her side as always.

Magda went to follow her but Kala stopped her. "Leave her be," she said, but she was looking at me.

"You stink of cow," Kala murmured to us. "What on earth have you been doing?"

"We were caught in a trap," Magda said bitterly. She raised her voice, turning to glare at me. "By his people."

Hounds all turned to me, baring their teeth. I was pitifully aware of my single set of fangs. I narrowed my eyes at Magda. I'd been raised to be nice to girls on principle but I still really wanted to kick her. I felt sure Byron or Shelley would have wanted to also.

"We didn't set the damn trap," I snapped. "Why would I go waltzing to a death trap if I knew it was there?"

"You weren't meant to be there at all," she said. "Your family could have set it without you knowing it."

"The Drakes didn't send the *Hel-Blar* after you." I seethed, my temper prickling. "We've treated you with every courtesy. I'm the one who was marked by some creepy-ass Hound spell."

It was funny how sharp silence could be, like a needle scraping against your skin.

Kala pushed herself up so she was sitting against a large rock painted with triple spirals.

"What mark, boy?"

"The dog paw," I told her. I was beginning to feel real concern. I hadn't had much time to think about it with the *Hel-Blar* attack and I kind of assumed it was just a scare tactic. I kept forgetting that this magic stuff might actually work.

Not a pleasant realization, actually.

"Do you have it on you?" Kala asked. Her eyes glittered, like ice breaking on a pond in spring.

"No."

"That will make it harder to break, but not impossible. Are you sure it was meant for you?"

"Isabeau said it had her mark on it."

"Are you accusing Isabeau?" Magda asked, incensed. "Do you see what royal loyalty is worth," she spat.

"I never accused Isabeau," I ground out. "I didn't even know it was her mark until she told me."

But she was already swinging her fist at me and it nearly collided. Disgusted surprise slowed my reflexes. She clipped my ear and I swung back and around. I didn't punch her, as punching girls, even crazy ones, wasn't cool. But I did trip her and I felt damn good about it.

"What the hell is your problem now?" I yelled at her.

"Isabeau is too good for you!" she yelled back. "And you'll take her away from us to live in your stupid royal house."

I was too stunned to duck the next blow. I barely felt it.

"I'm taking Isabeau home?" I echoed. "She forgot to tell me that part."

"Just like she forgot to tell *me* the bones said she'd find her mate in the royal family." She tried to snap my kneecap with her foot but I shoved her away.

"You're nuts," I told her. I couldn't deny I was intrigued though, couldn't deny I liked the idea of Isabeau promising herself to me and me to her. Even though I knew she was too prickly and independent to love me just because her shamanka told her to.

Still.

"Will you read the bones for me?" I asked Kala, ducking an empty urn Magda threw at my head. It broke into pieces against the wall. One of the dogs chased the shards, hoping for a treat. Kala wheezed a laugh.

"Come here, boy." She pulled a handful of painted bones out of a pouch at her belt. They looked like a cross between rune stones and spirals. I couldn't decipher them at all. She handed them to me. "Shake them in your cupped hands and then toss them on the ground between these two crystals." She thunked down two crystals.

"Kala, you're not well," Magda protested. "The royal pain can wait."

She had a point, much as I hated to admit it.

Kala only waved that away. "Throw!" she barked at me. I threw mostly out of reflex, the sharp whip of her voice startling me. Why were all the old ladies I knew so damn scary?

The bones tumbled and scattered on the dusty ground.

To Kala apparently they told a story. Some of the other Hounds edged closer, craning their heads for a better look. There were murmurs, a gasp. Magda scowled as if I'd just kicked a puppy. Kala nodded smugly.

"You see now? You all see. This is the boy."

I didn't see anything at all.

"You'll run with the dogs," she assured me, as if that was helpful. Then she coughed, bloody spittle on her lips.

"Leave her alone now," Magda snapped at me, gathering the stones up for Kala and turning her back to block me.

CHAPTER 14

Logan

I found Isabeau sitting on a rocky outcrop under the stars and a stunted pine tree. I climbed up toward her, dislodging pebbles under my boots. There was a behemoth sitting on her left, all fur and immensity.

"What the hell is that?" I asked.

"It's a dog," she replied matter-of-factly.

"Isabeau, that's not a dog, that's a moose."

She half smiled. "He's an English mastiff. His name is Ox-Eye."

Ox-Eye lifted his head. I'd seen smaller horses.

"Ox-Eye because he's part ox?" I asked, lowering into a crouch beside her.

"No, like the daisy."

"You named this beast after a flower?"

She scratched his ear fondly. "He's rather gentle. *Très sympathique.*"

"Sure he is," I said doubtfully. She was rubbing a piece of faded silk between her thumb and forefinger. It was frayed at the edges. "Good luck charm?" I asked softly.

She paused, slipped the cloth into her sleeve. "Yes, I suppose so. I thought I lost it a long time ago."

"What is it, Isabeau?" I asked.

"What do you mean?"

"Isabeau." I didn't know how I knew exactly, but I was sure there was something else going on. She bit her lower lip, finally looking like an eighteen-year-old girl.

"I was wearing that good luck charm, as you call it, the day I died. The day I was turned and left for dead, I should say." She sounded angry, bitter, and fragile in a way I hadn't thought was possible for her. It made me want to find the bastard and rip his head right off his shoulders. "I haven't seen it since that night."

I frowned. "Where did you find it?"

"In the woods outside your house," she replied. "When we were tracking the Host."

"Shit."

"*Oui.* It was left for me."

"By?"

"Greyhaven. Or so I assume. I was wearing it the night he killed me."

I sat back. "That's why you lost it when they said his name in the woods last night."

"*Oui*," she said again, grimly. "He's back. And now I can finally kill him."

"Isabeau, he's what, three hundred years old? Four hundred?"

"So?"

"So, you're a newborn, however long he might have left you in your grave." I really, really wanted to rip his head off. "You're not strong enough yet."

"We're not like other vampires, Logan," she insisted coolly.

"Yeah, believe me, I get that." I raised an eyebrow in her direction. What, did she think I was an idiot?

"I couldn't find Greyhaven before. He's always been off on Montmartre business. I couldn't get close to him, didn't even know if he was on the same continent." She pulled out the indigo silk. "But now I know. Now I can track him."

"How? I know you're good, Isabeau, but he's one of Montmartre's top lieutenants. Even I've heard his name."

"There are rituals."

I jerked a hand through my hair. "I'll just bet there are."

"I have this now. I can smell him on it."

"But why? Just to taunt you? There's something else going on here."

"I know," she admitted. "But I won't figure it out by sitting here and waiting for him to make his next move. What I can do is take this back to where I found it and dreamwalk."

"Dreamwalk?"

"Like a trance. Similar to what you saw with the cave paintings."

"And where exactly did you find it?"

She winced. "In the meadow where they set the trap."

My mouth dropped open. "In the field with the *Hel-Blar* and the blood everywhere? That's where you're going to lie down and go into a trance?"

"*Oui.*"

"Wow. That's the worst idea I've ever heard. And I've known Lucy practically her whole life."

"You don't understand."

I snorted. "I totally understand. You're nuts."

She shrugged one shoulder, let it fall. "I'm handmaiden to the shamanka. This is what I do."

"Ever notice you only say that when you're about to do something reckless?" The soft light from the setting moon caught the shiny skin of her numerous scars. "Did he give you those?" I was surprised that my voice sounded more like a growl. Ox-Eye lifted his head curiously.

"*Non*, the dogs did this."

I stared at her. "Your own dogs attacked you?"

"No." She smiled for the first time, softening the tight lines in her face. "They rescued me. Kala's dogs pulled me out of the earth. I would never have been able to do it by myself. Greyhaven only slipped me enough blood to change me, not enough to revive me. I was unconscious for centuries in that coffin."

"In France?"

"No, I was buried in London, in my uncle's family plot."

"And Kala went to get you?"

"No, she never leaves the mountains or these woods. It's her power center and the dogs are her totem, you would say. For all of us."

The only reason I could follow what she was saying was because of Lucy and her New Age parents. Lucy talked about totems and auras and full moon rituals the way other people talked about ballet classes and summer barbecues.

"So who found you?"

"She sent Finn across the ocean with three of her most trusted dogs. They have a way of calling other dogs to them. Finn told me that by the time he found me in Highgate cemetery nearly twenty of the city's stray dogs were there too."

I could picture it: mists, the middle of the night in a posh ancient graveyard in turn-of-the-century London under torchlight, the sound of horses and carriages over the wall. She'd have been wearing some kind of corseted gown with pearls at her throat and elbow-length gloves.

She was totally made for me.

"So the dogs found me and dug me out. I remember the sound of their claws and their teeth closing over my arms. And the air, finally, real air I could breathe. That's when I realized I wasn't actually breathing and I wasn't waking up from some nightmare in my uncle's townhouse in 1795. It was over two hundred years later and nothing made sense." She shivered, her eyes distant.

I'd thought our bloodchange was bad, but we knew it was coming and our family had had centuries to adapt and prepare. We got sick, sure, and weak, and some of us came closer to actually dying for real than others; but usually a draft of blood and we were right as rain. Vampiric, but otherwise okay and still ourselves in our recognizable undead life. In fact, Connor's real worry had been that he was going to have to start dressing like me. I'd given him a black velvet frock coat for his birthday that year and hung it on the back of his door so that it was the first thing he saw when he woke up.

"Finn gave me blood to drink," Isabeau continued. "I thought he was insane. He had to force me and I was sick all over his boots. After an hour I was so thirsty I would have drunk a barrel of blood. He brought me here as soon as I was well enough to travel, on a ship with a windowless bedroom and a captain who didn't ask questions. As soon as I saw Kala, I knew I was finally home."

I whistled. "So it's not just a story told to scare the rest of us?"

She shook her head. I reached out and traced a fingertip over a half-moon scar above her elbow. I half expected her to break my hand, or at least jerk away. She just went still.

"Your aunt thinks her scars make her hideous."

I went still as well. "You talked to my aunt Hyacinth?" I gaped. "And by that I mean, Aunt Hyacinth actually talked to someone?"

"Yes. She seems . . . distraught."

"That's one word for it. She's barely been out of her room since those rogue Helios-Ra bastards doused her in holy water and left her for dead. She won't talk to any of us, and she absolutely won't lift her veil. Not even for Uncle Geoffrey, and he's practically a doctor. You should have seen her before the attack. She was unstoppable, afraid of no one, and a bear about courtesy and proper gentlemanly behavior."

"So that's where you get it from."

"What?"

"The way you dress, the way you can bow like this is still the eighteenth century."

"I suppose." I shrugged, sternly telling myself not to ask her if she liked it or hated it. I wasn't going to be that guy.

"If you had dug me out instead of Finn, I might not have realized right away that it wasn't still the eighteenth century."

Ordinarily, I'd take that as a great compliment; with her though, I just wasn't sure.

"Between our matriarch, Madame Veronique, and her medieval lessons and Aunt Hyacinth, I guess it was bound to rub off on one of us."

"You're different than your brothers," Isabeau insisted. "They don't live it the way you do. I could tell right away."

"You noticed all that in the few hours you saw them?" And I absolutely wasn't going to wonder who she'd thought was the cutest. Quinn had a way around girls, and it made them stupid. I suddenly wanted to punch him for it.

"No, it's kind of nice," she murmured, and suddenly Quinn's face was safe from my fist. "It's like the boys I knew in France."

I wasn't entirely thrilled with the word "boy."

"I didn't know I missed it," she continued, as if surprising herself.

I'd never wanted anything more than I wanted to kiss her. I

wanted it more than I lusted after Christina Ricci in *Sleepy Hollow*. And I'm all about the girls in corsets. Isabeau's long, thick black hair, straight as the waterfall in the caves underneath us, her green eyes and scarred arms and vicious parry with a sword. Hot. Every last bit of her.

I decided to take my own life in my hands and I leaned in slowly. I didn't rush, gave her plenty of time to pull away, but I was inexorably closing the distance between us. She smelled like rain and earth and wine. If she'd been in a goblet I would have drained it of every drop. I was a whisper away from her now and she still hadn't moved.

I wanted to bury my hands in her hair and draw her up against me but I thought she might not be ready for that. She was a little bit like a wild animal, untamed, unbroken, and as untethered as a hawk in the sky. I wouldn't want her to be anything else.

I slanted my lips over hers and it felt right, necessary. I kissed her deeply, slowly, as if we had all the time in the world. Her mouth opened and her tongue touched mine, hesitantly, sweetly. I had to clench my fists to keep from grabbing her. The kiss went darker, wilder—one of us made a small sound but I honestly didn't know which of us it was.

There was a tingle in the back of my head, a flush of burning heat over my entire body. I pulled away reluctantly. Her mouth quirked into one of her rare smiles.

"Dawn," she whispered.

I smoothed her swollen lower lip with my thumb. "Dawn," I agreed.

The forest was ever so slightly less dark than it had been, more gray than black.

"We should go inside," she said, both sets of fangs protruding slightly. It was cute as hell.

"Got someplace safe for me to sleep?" I asked.

She linked her fingers through mine.

"Yes."

Chapter 15

Logan

"Have I mentioned that this is the worst idea ever?"

"A hundred times." Isabeau rolled her eyes. Charlemagne looked like he was considering it too.

"If I say it a hundred and one times will it convince you?"

"No." She ducked under a low-hanging branch. "You fret worse than my old nursemaid."

"I have a great deal of sympathy for your old nursemaid," I muttered. It was a beautiful night, warm and filled with stars and the songs of crickets and frogs. White flowers glowed in the grass. It was a night made for poetry. We should have been kissing. A lot.

Instead we were sneaking out of the caves to a blood-soaked clearing where we'd been ambushed not twenty-four hours earlier. Not exactly an ordinary date.

"It will be fine," she assured me, her long black hair swinging behind her. "It's just trancework, nothing to worry about."

"Really?" I answered dryly. "Is that why we snuck out and you wouldn't tell anyone what we're doing, not even Magda?"

"I don't want to worry them. And they wouldn't understand, anyway."

"*I* don't understand," I shot back.

"I know. But you're still here, you're still helping. You're not trying to stop me."

I shook my head. "I am so trying to stop you—I'm just doing a piss-poor job of it, apparently."

When I woke up next to Isabeau in her cave, her hand on my chest, I'd thought the night would go rather differently. I should have known better. There was nothing soft about Isabeau, not even in her sleep. Well, that wasn't precisely true. I'd seen a flash of her vulnerability, after all, a flash I didn't think she was even aware she possessed. She was all shamanka's handmaiden out of the caves, all warrior and duty. But this was her home and she was comfortable enough to shed a few of her hard outer layers.

Her room had been simple, nearly sparse. There was a futon covered in quilts and several dog beds in the corners, thick rugs, and a small oil painting of a French vineyard. There were no concert posters or a closet stuffed with dresses, just a hope chest for her clothes, another one for weapons, and a jewelry box filled with amulets and bone beads. Everything about her was different.

And she'd ruined me for regular girls.

Even now, as she stalked through the forest, hypervigilant for the stench of *Hel-Blar* or a sneak attack from the Host.

"We're close," she murmured.

"I know." I could feel the stinging in my nostrils, the penny-sharp tang of dried blood. Broken glass glittered in the undergrowth. Charlemagne sniffed his way around the clearing and then sat, tongue lolling out of the corner of his mouth. Clearly, we were alone. What a waste of a moonlit night.

She frowned at the ground. "Look, dog prints."

I followed her gaze to the trampled grass, the paw marks. "Charlemagne?"

"No, there are too many. And they're fresh."

I took a closer look. "Someone came back here after we left, just to add dog prints?" I rocked back on my heels, chilled. "To frame the Hounds for the attacks, same as the death charm in my pocket."

She nodded tersely. "Montmartre, probably."

"He doesn't want the treaties," I agreed. "He'd much prefer we fight each other than him." I sighed. "So, what now?"

She was walking the perimeter much as Charlemagne had, her head tilted, sniffing delicately. "Now for the ritual."

I frowned. "Are you sure about this? Montmartre could be anywhere. And I didn't even know magic was actually real before your trick with the love charm."

She shook her head, mystified. The bone beads in her hair clattered together. "I'll never understand how vampires could be so ignorant of the magic in their own veins, in their own bodies."

I shrugged uncomfortably.

"I can do this, Logan," she said confidently. "Kala trained me for this."

"What if something goes wrong? I can't exactly wave a magic wand over you. I'm not Harry Potter."

"Who?"

"Never mind," I said.

"All you have to do to pull me out is say my name three times. If that doesn't work, bury both my hands in the earth."

"I'm not even going to ask."

"It will ground me back into my body. Honestly, what does your family teach you?"

She pulled dried herbs out of a pouch hanging from her belt and scattered the mixture in the center of the meadow. I could smell mint, clove, peppercorn, and something unfamiliar. She'd put a new amulet around her neck: this one was tarnished silver and hung with tiny bells and garnet beads like frozen drops of blood. There were symbols etched around the edges.

Next she pulled what looked like tibia bones out of her pack and stuck them into the dirt. They were smooth and polished and painted with more symbols. One was wrapped in copper wire and pearls.

"Are those human?" I frowned. Vampires didn't leave bones behind, only ashes.

"Dog," she replied. "And wolf."

"Oh." I didn't know what else to say to that.

She lay down on her back between the bones, one at her head, one at her feet. The trees around us glimmered with broken bottles. Her arms were bare as usual, scars proudly displayed, chain mail draped over her heart. She closed her eyes, looking like a feral Sleeping Beauty.

I unsheathed my sword and paced slowly around her, listening so intently for sounds of another ambush that sweat gathered under my hair. She shifted, making herself more comfortable and murmured something too softly for me to hear.

She lay there for a long time, quietly and eerily still.

Just as I was beginning to think there was nothing more magical happening than a nap, every nerve ending tingled and the hairs on my arms stirred. It suddenly felt like I was entirely covered in static electricity.

I turned to Isabeau, sword swinging out protectively.

She was alone, safe. But I could have sworn a silver glow pushed out of her skin, making her shine. She didn't seem concerned; in fact she smiled, the corner of her mouth lifting slightly. I admit I was relieved. I wasn't exactly sure how to go about fighting an invisible enemy.

There were clearly gaps in the famous Drake education.

I could just imagine what Mom would have to say about that.

And then the grass around her flattened outward in a circle, as if pushed by a strong wind. When it hit me, I staggered back, hitting a tree. A bottle fell from a branch overhead and tipped blood into the grass. I straightened, cursing.

Isabeau stood up as well. She seemed to be glowing even more than before. It was a little distracting.

"I guess it didn't work," I told her.

She blinked at me. "Actually, it worked a little too well."

I was beginning to notice that everything around me seemed insubstantial, faded. And that I appeared to be glowing a little bit too, like those nature films about incandescent phloem under the surface of the sea. "I don't think I want to know what you mean by that."

"You're dreamwalking with me, Logan."

"Yup, that's what I didn't want to know."

She looked confused. "This has never happened before."

"Yeah, that's the opposite of comforting." I could see through my hand.

Not good.

I tried to clench my fingers tighter around the sword. Everything glittered around the edges, like the night sky was reaching down to touch everything. In fact, the sky seemed closer than it ought to be.

"Put that away," Isabeau told me. "It won't do you any good anyway. Weapons are useless when just a wayward thought can kill."

"Well, shit, that's just great."

"The best weapon's a mirror."

"Huh?" I was only half paying attention.

"So you can see a person's true face. Don't trust appearances here, Logan, any more than you would in your regular body."

"Okay, sure." The trees had a green glow, pulsing slowly like a heartbeat. In fact, everything seemed to have some kind of bright, candy-colored aura. "Did you slip some of that mushroom tea into my blood supply when I woke up?"

"No, this is perfectly normal," she assured me.

"Right," I countered dubiously.

"Well, not exactly normal," she amended. "I've never taken someone into a dreamwalk with me before."

"I feel totally weird," I told her, staring at my body, which was shooting off sparks.

"You'll get used to it. We should hurry though, it's not good to stay too long on your first journey."

"Why?"

"You might turn into a toad."

I gaped at her in horror, tried to stutter a reply but couldn't form the words. It took a full two minutes for me to realize she was joking. She actually chuckled out loud.

"Oh, sure, now you giggle like a girl. You have a sadistic sense of humor."

She grinned, unfazed. "You're not the first to say so."

I turned, saw myself leaning against the tree, lace cuffs spilling out of my sleeves, sword tip resting in a clump of violets. It was like the near-death experiences people talked about on all those psychic shows. Only I was already technically dead. I wasn't moving and my eyes were open, watching nothing. "Okay, that's just creepy."

"Don't look at yourself for too long," she suggested. "It'll make you queasy."

"I can see why." I turned away deliberately. "So now what?"

"Now we hunt for psychic traces, for anything that looks out of place, anything with an absence of light or a strange scent."

The blood from the bottle traps was a different color, like I was looking at a photographic negative. It was molten silver and it made everything else look darker, more translucent. Isabeau was crouched, sifting through the undergrowth with her fingers, plucking bits of broken glass as if they were petals off a flower. I tried not to be distracted by the way her eyes went green as mint leaves, by the way the stars seemed to leak light, by the hundreds of spiders and beetles and moths moving all around us.

She shoved to her feet, wiping her hands. "Nothing," she said, frustrated.

I paid closer attention to our surroundings, to the scents. I could smell mud and the river and pine needles and the humming off Isabeau's skin. And aside from the fact that everything looked like it was covered in glow-in-the-dark paint, it was all pretty normal. Footsteps, scuffs in the dirt, all the marks of our battle in the proper places.

Except.

I paused. The spot where Jen had disintegrated was dull, as if the shimmering light had dried to powder. I felt sick to my stomach.

"Isabeau."

She hurried over, startled at my tone. "What is it?" She stopped. "Oh. A violent death leaves psychic marks that can take years to fade," she said quietly.

"But she's not stuck here, right?" I asked sharply. "This is just residue?"

She nodded. "*Oui*."

I released the breath I would have been holding if I'd still been able to breathe. "Okay. Good." She had a weird look on her face, her nostrils flaring. "Isabeau?"

"I didn't notice before," she murmured. If vampires could go green with nausea, she would have.

"What, damn it?"

"It wasn't just cow blood in the bottles," she said. "Montmartre's blood was in there as well. Just enough to be certain the *Hel-Blar* would follow the scent."

I frowned. "You know, that doesn't exactly make a lot of sense. Just once I'd like an answer, not more questions. We know Montmartre is after Solange, and he's making sure the rest of us don't negotiate a treaty. We can assume Greyhaven is doing his dirty work here, but that still doesn't explain why he has it in for you."

"I would really like to kill him," Isabeau said, as if she was asking for a second eclair at the local cafe.

I nodded at her amulets. "Um, you're sparking."

She looked down, blinking. The amulet was like the tooth that had broken when we'd heard about the attack on Kala. It was polished and capped with silver and small crystals that shot off a fountain of light, like a Fourth of July sparkler.

"*Bien,*" she said, slipping the necklace off and wrapping the chain around her wrist so that the dog tooth dangled over her thumb. She stretched her arm out, watching it turn in circles, clockwise and then counterclockwise. I'd seen Lucy use a pendulum once in the same way, only she'd been trying to find out where her mother had hidden her birthday presents.

"There's something here," she said. "A connection I am missing." She stalked the perimeter with concentrated purpose, frowning into the grass, at the trees, spending extra time over the remains of the bottles. She stopped, swore fervently and fluently. It was all in French but there was no mistaking her tone. She dug a shard of green glass out of an exposed oak tree root.

"What is it?" I asked, grabbing for my sword, even though she'd assured me it was useless.

"I know this," she said, peeling the painted yellowed label with her thumbnail. Her eyes went dangerously watery, then brittle. "This is from my family vineyard."

I took a step toward her. "It's definitely personal," I said darkly.

"*Oui.*"

"Why?"

"I really don't know."

I hated how shattered she looked. "Greyhaven is playing you, trying to get under your skin."

"*Oui.*"

"Don't let him, Isabeau." I grabbed her shoulders, squeezed hard until she stopped staring at the wine bottle fragment and blinked up at me. "Don't you let that son of a bitch win."

There was a long moment when I wondered what she would do next. She was utterly unpredictable.

"You're right. He's doing this for a reason." Her chin tilted up and she was the Isabeau I'd first met: fierce, hard, and a little bit terrifying. "So I have to find out what that reason is."

"*We* have to find out," I corrected her, just as grimly. "You're not alone."

"Of course I am." She smiled wistfully, but she unclenched her fingers from the shard. Blood welled on her skin, but it was silver.

I'd assumed you couldn't be physically hurt when you were astral traveling or whatever the hell it was we were doing. It seemed only fair.

She frowned at the silvery blood. "*Non*," she squeaked. She dropped the shard, frantically wiped her hands clean, even wiped her fingers on her pants until they were raw.

"*Merde.*"

And then her eyes rolled back in her head and she crumpled.

CHAPTER 16

Paris, 1793

After the food riots broke out, Isabeau took to the rooftops of Paris.

She'd scrambled up to the sturdy roof of a *fromagerie* to get away from the horde of starving Parisians and local villagers as they stormed the cobbled streets with bayonets, pitchforks, and torches. Her favorite *patisserie*, the one the revolutionaries never bothered with and whose owner often gave her stale croissants, burned to the ground in a matter of minutes. Thick black smoke filled the air; coughing and cursing filled the alleys. The fire traveled next door to the tooth puller and crept too close to a popular café. Buckets of water were hauled and passed hand to hand. Isabeau dropped back to the ground to help, pulling her collar up over her face. She wore the workmen trousers of the revolutionaries and a tricolor cockade on her hat. She'd put up her hair and tried to affect a lower voice when she spoke, which was rarely. She'd learned quickly that looking like a boy and spouting *"Fraternite"* whenever anyone asked her a direct question was the surest way to stay unnoticed and uninteresting. A girl with an aristocratic accent, soft hands, and long hair would never survive.

And her father had died so she could survive.

So she would survive.

However much she might want otherwise.

It was the end of February and the streets were slick with rain and cold, the smoke clinging in doorways. The fire raged, as hungry as the rioters. Isabeau crept closer, closed her eyes at the feel of the warmth on her face. She didn't move back until a rafter broke and hung over the alley, dropping burning wattle and wood. Her hands felt warm for the first time in a month. Even with the burn on her thumb it was worth it.

She was jostled aside. More water arced into the flames and they sputtered indignantly. It wasn't long before the *patisserie* was a pile of smoldering embers, the dark-haired owner yelling obscenities from across the street.

When the *gendarmes* arrived, Isabeau slunk away. It hadn't taken her long to learn to avoid anyone in power: police, a magistrate, even the night watchman who sat under a streetlight and drank wine until he fell asleep, snoring into his chest. The urchins liked to set spiders on his hair and run away giggling.

She hauled herself back up onto a nearby roof and flattened herself down, staying out of sight. She tucked her fingers into the frayed cuffs of her shirt. It was safe up here, quiet. There were only pigeons to contend with and the odd skinny cat. She could walk along the roofline from one end of town to the other, as long as she took care to avoid the poorer sections where the roof might give out altogether. She could eavesdrop on the revolutionaries shouting amiably at each other in the cafe and the beat of the drums from La Place de la Concorde when another prisoner was dragged up to the guillotine. She couldn't stand to watch the executions; just listening to the crowds chanting and those drums made her ill.

A few hours later when her stomach was grumbling louder than the quashed rioters, she slid down a spout and landed nimbly in an alley that stunk of urine and rose water. Once the sun went down, the prostitutes would lounge at the corner, winking at the men. She had an hour yet before it was dark enough that she had to find a rooftop.

She hunched her shoulders and kept her eyes on the ground as she turned onto the crowded pavement. Horses trundled past, their hooves clicking loudly on the stones. Someone had set a fire to blazing in a iron cauldron outside a cafe. She slowed her pace, casting a surreptitious glance at the abandoned plates for uneaten food. One of the servers glowered, flicking his fingers at her. She'd become an unwashed, faceless street urchin who drove away customers. It seemed like ages ago that she been choosing brocade for a new gown and wondering when she was going to be betrothed, and to whom and if he would be kind and still have all his own teeth. Now she smelled like dirt and mildewed roof shingles. She grimaced.

"Such a face on such a pretty girl."

Isabeau froze, then hunched her shoulders more.

"You'll never pass for a boy if you keep walking like that, *chouette*."

Isabeau turned her head slightly. The prostitute smiled at her. One of her teeth was missing and her cheeks were rouged enough to resemble apples.

"I don't know what you mean," Isabeau said as hoarsely as she could. She spit on the ground for good measure and only barely avoided her own foot.

"Better," the prostitute approved. "But you need to take bigger steps, as if you're ready to fight anyone who gets in your way."

"I don't want to fight," she protested, alarmed.

"And you won't have to if everyone thinks you want to."

"I'm not sure that makes sense."

She grinned. "Sense doesn't have a lot to do with being a man." Her bosom was dangerously close to spilling right out of her stained corset. Her long skirt was tucked up to her hip, showing stockings with several runs and a sturdy, sensible pair of boots. The contradiction made Isabeau blink. "My name's Cerise," the woman introduced herself.

"I'm . . . Arnaud."

"Not a bad name," Cerise said. "But you might do better with something more common, like Alain."

"Oh." She couldn't believe she was spitting and talking to a prostitute. The old Isabeau would have sniffed a lace handkerchief soaked in lavender oil to cover the scents of this place if she'd ridden by in her family carriage. She wouldn't even have noticed Cerise with her cold-chapped hands and frizzy hair. Isabeau shivered when the wind sliced around the corner.

"You need a coat."

She shrugged. "I'm all right." She clamped her back teeth together so they wouldn't chatter.

"Mmm-hmmm," Cerise said dryly. "If you follow the cart down to the river, that's where they dump the bodies after executions."

Isabeau swallowed thickly. Cerise patted her shoulder. "It's better than freezing to death."

Isabeau wasn't convinced, but she'd been raised to be polite. "Thank you," she replied cautiously.

"If you go now, you might catch it before it's picked clean."

Isabeau nodded and pulled her collar up to cover the back of her neck.

"And *cherie*?" Cerise called after her. "Stay away from the cafe at the end of the street. It's not safe for young girls or young boys."

"Thank you," she said again. This time it was more heartfelt.

She found herself walking down to the river, even though the thought of robbing a decapitated body made bile rise in the back of her throat. The truth was, she didn't have a single coin to her name and nothing worth selling aside from a scrap of silk from her mother's favorite gown. It probably wasn't enough to buy her a meal and she wouldn't have sold it regardless. It was all she had left of her parents, her home, and her real life.

She spotted the cart a few streets over, wheels creaking as it rumbled down toward the Seine. Most of the shopkeepers didn't even bother looking up from their work. Children and dogs chased after it singing a song Isabeau had never heard before. It sounded like an old lullaby but the words were obscene. The cart jerked over a broken cobblestone and an arm flopped over the side. Isabeau gagged but somehow kept walking. The rain started to fall fitfully, more like ice pellets than a gentle spring shower. It was still winter. She shivered violently, tried to tell herself that her shirt was thick enough to keep her warm, she just had to get used to the cold. She was soft, too accustomed to fireplaces and hot stew and mulled wine at any hour of the day or night.

The river moved sluggishly, as if it were too cold to do its work as well. She knew mill wheels would be creaking farther down the flow, in the villages. There'd been a wheel just like it near her parents' country house. Here the river was muddy and ordered with a broken stone wall.

Isabeau wasn't the only one easing out of the alleys as the cart stopped at the bank. She tried to tell herself to turn around and find herself a hidden rooftop where she could warm her hands in the smoke out of the chimney. Instead, she watched, frozen, as the two men began tossing severed heads into the river. Blood dripped into the dirt under the cart wheels. Bodies were rolled down into the gray water. There were half a dozen of them. Then the men got back up onto the cattle cart and urged the horse into a walk.

Isabeau leaped over the wall and crept along its broken stones like rotten teeth, keeping low. A head bobbed in the icy water, spinning to grimace at her with a grotesque leer. She stuffed her fist into her mouth to keep from screaming. She felt light-headed, as if she wasn't in her body. She watched herself approach a headless corpse caught on the bank and turn it over. It had been a man once, slender enough that his coat would fit her. It was dark gray and wool, already missing all its buttons. There was only a small tear in one shoulder and it was relatively free of blood. The scarf he was wearing had sopped most of it up.

She couldn't think of it. She could only keep moving, like a marionette, aware only of the frigid wind and the way her fingernails were turning blue with cold. The other bodies were being picked over by a gang of young boys and a girl no older than five who kept demanding something shiny. She had to be quick. She yanked and pulled until the coat was free, tears freezing in her eyelashes. She slipped it on and then ran back into the alleys, stopping only to retch in a dark corner before hauling herself up onto a roof.

The sun sank slowly, bleeding red and purple light over the city.

By the time spring unfurled its tender green buds on all the treetops, Isabeau had learned the layout of the streets, and thanks to Cerise, which neighborhoods to avoid altogether, even in daylight. She'd found a jar of olives packed in oil and spinach leaves left over at the market. They were only a little bit trampled and reminded her of the spinach and garlic sauce Cook used to make for special occasions. She ate them with her fingers, crouched on the roof of a bookshop. She'd stopped seeing the bodies on the riverbank every time she closed her eyes and was grateful for the warmth of the coat when the rains started.

She saved the last few olives and tucked the jar in her pocket, swinging down to the ground. If there had been a carnival around, she liked to think she could have been an acrobat or a tightrope walker. She gave wide berth to a cafe known for its political squabbles and ducked under a creaking sign of an apothecary. The chain had snapped in last night's storm and the sign was swinging drunkenly, banging into the wooden frame around the window. She found Cerise leaning out of the window of the room she shared with five other prostitutes.

"Fancy a go, *citoyen?*" A thin woman with bruises on her arms smiled at her. Isabeau took a startled step backward.

"Never mind him, Francine," Cerise called down. "He's here for me."

"You get all the clean pretty ones." Francine pouted, wandering away.

Isabeau was embarrassed right down to her toes. Cerise laughed loudly.

"I forget how young you are sometimes," she said.

Isabeau made a face at her and used the sagging counter of a fishmonger's to boost herself up to Cerise's porch. It was more of a wooden ledge outside a broken window than an actual proper porch, but it did the trick.

"What did you bring me this time?" Cerise asked eagerly. Her roommates were snoring loudly in the darkened room behind them. She looked tired, the lines around her eyes were deeper. Isabeau sometimes forgot she was a couple of years younger than her own mother had been when she was born. Amandine had retained a kind of childlike innocence that Cerise had likely outgrown by the time she'd lost her last baby tooth.

"Here." Isabeau handed her the olives.

Cerise clutched it. "I haven't had olives in weeks."

"I've got something even better," Isabeau assured her, fishing out another treasure from her inside pocket, wrapped in old butcher's paper. She'd stolen it from the back garden of a fancy townhouse a street away from her parents' old house.

Cerise goggled when Isabeau pulled the paper back. "Are those . . . ?"

Isabeau nodded, sliding the bundle into Cerise's trembling fingers. "Strawberries."

"I've never had strawberries before."

"Eat them quickly or you'll have to share."

Cerise stuffed them into her mouth before her roommates could stir and ask about the sweet sugary smell. Her eyes closed as if she were eating chocolate mousse for the first time.

"Heavenly," she declared in a soft voice. Tiny seeds stuck between her teeth.

"I knew you'd like them." The sun was high overhead, hot for the first time since the autumn. Isabeau turned her face up to it. "I can't wait for summer."

"Marc told me to tell you that they're having a big rally in La Place de la Concorde today."

Isabeau looked at her hopefully. "How big a rally?"

"He said you could work it with your eyes closed. He's never seen anyone with fingers as nimble as yours." She waggled her eyebrows. "I wager he could think of better ways to occupy those dainty hands of yours."

"Cerise!" Isabeau lowered her voice. "You didn't tell him I'm a girl, did you?"

"No, *chouette*. He definitely thinks you're a boy."

"Then why would he be interested in . . ." She trailed off, confused.

Cerise laughed so hard she choked. "Never mind, I'll tell you later." She wiped her eyes. "How have you survived this long?"

"Because of you," Isabeau replied seriously.

Cerise wiped her eyes more vigorously. "You'll make me cry."

"Why did you help me, Cerise?" Isabeau had always wanted to ask but she hadn't wanted to frighten off the only friend she had. One didn't ask questions in the back alleys.

"I had a daughter once," Cerise replied, her voice so soft it was nearly drowned out by the squawk of pigeons pecking at the weeds at the side of the building. "She would have been about your age now."

"What happened to her?"

"She caught a fever one winter when she was still a baby. I couldn't afford medicine. When I broke the window of the apothecary to steal some, the *gendarmes* took me off to Bastille. She died before they let me out again."

Isabeau bit her lip. "I'm sorry."

Cerise nodded, touched the tiny glass drop earrings she never took off. "That's why I wear these."

"That's glass from the Bastille, isn't it?" It had become fashionable to wear rings and jewelry set with stones or glass from the Bastille, to commemorate the storming of the jail four years earlier.

She nodded fiercely. "Yes, I was never so happy as the day we pulled that prison apart." She swallowed harshly, shook her head. "Enough of that now, it doesn't do to live in the past." She squinted at the position of the sun. "You'd best hurry if you're going to make the square in time."

Isabeau hauled herself up onto the roof, poked her head back down.

"What do you want today, Cerise?" she asked, forcing a note of cheer into her voice.

"A ribbon for my corset," Cerise suggested, smiling again. It had become a game, to see what odd trinket Isabeau could find for her, once she'd finished working the crowd for more serious wares.

Isabeau hurried along the rooftops, following the sounds of the political rally. As promised, the square bulged with people, children, dogs, and cheese vendors hoping for a sale. The rain had washed the cobblestones and the streets clear, and the wind carried off the stench of so many unwashed bodies and the garbage in the alleys. There was a man at the podium dressed in the trousers favored by revolutionaries instead of the aristocratic knee breeches—thus the name "*sans-culottes*." He had the tricolor cockade pinned to his hat, just as Isabeau did. Almost everyone in Paris wore one, even if they were secretly royalists. Everyone wanted to avoid unwanted attention. It was the only way to survive the riots and the National Guard and the *gendarmes* and revolutionaries.

He was yelling passionately about *Fraternite* and *Liberte* and state education for children. Isabeau didn't pay much attention to what he was saying. She wasn't here to join the cause, or even to fight against it. She was here solely for the coin she could lift from unattended pockets. She had a small stash tucked under the roof shingle of a ribbon shop that saw few customers these days. Soon, if the summer was kind to her, she would have enough to buy passage on a ship to England. If she went before winter, she could walk from the shore to London, to find her uncle's house. She was trying to convince Cerise to go with her but the other woman absolutely refused to leave France, and spat at the mention of England.

Isabeau used her high vantage point to scope out the movement of the crowd, where it clogged together and where it thinned out. Once she'd marked her best point of entry, she leaped down into an alley, scaring a cat and neatly avoiding a puddle of unidentified liquid. She strolled casually toward the main part of the square, looking for all the world as if she were paying close attention to the speeches. Someone handed her a flyer.

She let herself be jostled, stepped on a foot and apologized profusely. The man shrugged her off, checking his pockets. They were gratifyingly full and he forgot her instantly. The man next to him didn't think to check and she hid a smile, dropping the silver coin she'd filched from his coat. She'd hung her coat on a chimney and practiced for days until she could pick her own pockets without even disturbing the pigeons nesting above it. She was proud of herself, as proud as she'd been the day she'd played her first song at the piano without a single pause or mistake. Prouder even then when she'd earned the praises of her dancing master.

Anyone could learn to dance.

Picking pockets was a harder skill to learn and eminently more useful.

By the end of the square she'd amassed another silver coin, a copper chain with a broken clasp, a bag of walnuts, and a feather from a woman's bonnet. She'd have to find a red ribbon later. If she stayed any longer she increased the chances of being discovered. Greed would get her killed.

She spotted Marc leaning against a pillar, his dirty face half-hidden under a cap. He winked at her as she passed but otherwise made no sign that he knew her. She slipped him the copper chain as a thank-you, nicked a clump of radishes from a basket, and vanished onto the maze of shingles and broken chimneys above the city.

CHAPTER 17

Logan

"What the hell was that?" I choked as we were tossed back into the clearing. We weren't in 1793 Paris anymore, but we weren't in our bodies yet either. We shimmered like ghosts over the grass, our bodies slumped several feet away. I couldn't get the image of Isabeau, abandoned and orphaned, clinging to rooftops.

"That's never happened before," Isabeau murmured, startled and embarrassed.

"You know, you keep saying that."

She swallowed, turning away slightly as if she was embarrassed to look at me. That was definitely new. "So now you know what I was."

I blinked. "Resourceful, clever, self-sufficient. Same as now."

She blinked back. "Logan, weren't you paying attention? I robbed corpses and picked pockets."

"You survived." There wasn't an ounce of censure in my voice, except maybe at the suggestion that I would think less of her.

"I was no better than Madame Tussaud," she said, disgusted.

"What does this have to do with wax museums?"

"I'm talking about Madame Tussaud, who made death masks. I read that she dug through the corpses of the guillotine victims to find decapitated heads for her masks. What are you talking about?"

"A tourist attraction. They make wax replicas of famous people. I guess it was named after your Madame Tussaud."

"This century is just odd," she muttered.

"This from a girl who survived the French Revolution."

"We're blue already," she murmured. That's when I noticed the glow we were emanating was brighter, slightly blue around the hazy edges. "We don't have much time left, we'll need to get back into our bodies before our spirits forget the way."

"I do feel kind of odd." Like the pull of my body was warring with the pull to just float away.

"Are you all right? I still need to get a connection to Montmartre." She kneeled and wiped her hands in the silver blood. "Which I can do, with this." Her palms were smeared with thick silver, like oil paint. Her teeth were clenched tight together as she dabbed the metallic blood on her forehead, between her eyebrows. She wavered, as if I were looking at her through heat lightning. She was going to vanish again and I wasn't touching her this time. Hell if I was going to stay behind and float. I grabbed her hand, the blood cool on my skin.

"Dangerous," she croaked, fading.

"Shut up," I croaked back, suddenly feeling a wicked jolt of vertigo. This wasn't like watching a memory out of her head, this was being pulled into a different place and not knowing where that place was. Everything was a bleary smear of colors, then black, then a painful thump on the head.

"Ouch, damn it."

We were in real time, pressed against the ceiling of a house, as if gravity had reversed itself. For all I knew, it had. She was practically vibrating with rage. I was trying not to throw up. Could disembodied spirits throw up? Best not to think about it.

"Look," she said, her voice nearly hollow with pain.

Below us was a lavish living room with a bar with a green marble countertop and bottles of blood lined up like vintage wines. A human woman wept in the corner, curled into a ball, blood staining her wrists and the inside crease of her elbows. Two guards were stationed at the main doorway in the Hosts' customary brown leather, and another two at the back door, which led out to a flagstone patio. In the center of the room, Montmartre reclined in a leather chair, looking like a dark prince out of some movie. His black hair was tied back, his eyes unnaturally pale. The last time I'd seen him he'd been trying to abduct my unconscious baby sister.

I cast Isabeau a sidelong glance, tried to keep my tone light. "If you keep grinding your teeth like that your fangs will break right off."

She wasn't smiling but at least she didn't look like someone was driving nails through her skull anymore.

"Can they hear us?" I asked.

She shook her head. "Only a witch or a shamanka could hear us now and they have neither down there."

"Finally, a bit of luck. Rat bastard," I hissed down at Montmartre. "Mangy dog of a scurvy goat."

"That doesn't even make sense," Isabeau murmured.

"Feels good though. Try it."

She narrowed her eyes at the top of Montmartre's perfectly groomed hair. "Balding donkey's ass. "

"Nice."

"Sniveling flea-bitten rabid monkey droppings."

"Clearly, you're a natural." I frowned. "Why is he glowing red?"

"You're seeing his aura," Isabeau explained. "It's easier to see when you're in this state. And that particular shade of red is unique to him. Do you see the guards there? Their auras are unique as well, but there's a tinge of red, on the outside." She was right. They looked like hazy jawbreaker candy, all layers of color. "It marks them as Montmartre's tribes."

"Wait, so we all have that?" I couldn't help but notice that Isabeau's aura and mine were the same shifting glimmer of blue-opal, all along the side of our bodies that were nearly touching.

"Yes."

"What color are the Drakes'?"

"Blue-gray, like the surface of a lake when a storm's coming. Lucy's is very, very pink, like cotton candy. The *Hel Blar* have an absence of color, which makes my head hurt."

"This really doesn't get less weird, does it?"

The guards saluted and moved aside before she could reply.

Another man strode into the room, dressed in a ridiculously expensive designer suit. His hair was dark brown and artlessly styled, the kind of careless style you have to work really hard at. He wasn't very tall, too soft and aristocratic to look threatening, if it weren't for the sinister power that all but leaked out of his pores. I drifted closer to Isabeau. I felt the sudden need to protect her, floating delicately above two predators who'd already tried to kill her more than once. I didn't recognize the new vampire, but my mother hadn't raised an idiot.

"Greyhaven?" I whispered.

She nodded once, brokenly, like a doll with a wooden neck. I wanted to hold her even more than I wanted to get back into my body. Neither was an immediate option.

Greyhaven mixed blood and brandy into a glass and threw the contents back before speaking.

"The *Hel-Blar* are causing a nice distraction," he said. The sound of his voice had Isabeau jerking back as if he'd tried to stake her.

Montmartre didn't look particularly impressed. He looked exhausted actually, nearly gray with fatigue. Good.

"We got the package in through sheer luck," he said. "We don't have the time or the men to launch an attack on the Drake farm. We'd need the element of surprise and we can't get it, not now. And they won't let the blasted girl out."

They were talking about Solange. There was a weird growling sound I didn't realized was coming from my own throat until I nearly choked on it.

"She'll be at the coronation," Greyhaven assured him smoothly. "You can grab her then. And the crown."

"Yes, because that worked so well for me the last time," he said dryly.

"You worry too much."

"They'll be expecting us at the coronation," Montmartre said, rising to his feet. "We'll have to act faster than that. I can get the girl once I have the crown." He smiled and it sent a chill through me. "Get your men ready. We'll send in the human guards before sunset tomorrow and follow them."

"But . . ." Montmartre didn't see the odd look on Greyhaven's face, but I could see it clearly enough. And I had no idea how to interpret it; it was tense, hopeful, sad, angry, jealous, adoring. Too much, too fast for one expression. And it was washed over with a thin veneer of panic. Clearly Greyhaven wasn't the spontaneous sort. He didn't like having the plans changed.

Since those plans involved killing my family and marrying my little sister against her will, he could bite me.

"We have to warn them," I said to Isabeau. Suddenly, hovering like a waft of mist was extremely annoying. I was too angry and tense and worried to float; I wanted to feel the ground under my boots as I thundered through the woods to the royal caves. I wanted the hilt of a good sword in my hand, the smooth deadly grip of a stake. Now.

Greyhaven frowned lightly and peered suspiciously into the dark corners of the room.

"*Merde*." Isabeau reached for me before I could reach for her.

Her fingers dug into my arm. "Think of your body," she whispered, her mouth so close to my ear it tickled the lobe. Greyhaven's head jerked up and then we were shimmering through another bout of vertigo. I had no idea if he'd seen us. I had no idea which way was up and which was down. I hurtled through the air for what felt like years and then landed in a lump right beside my body. I looked decidedly more peaceful than I felt.

Isabeau looked utterly shell-shocked, as if her astral limbs were heavy as stones. Her aura flickered, like a lightbulb about to burn out.

"Hey," I said gently, pushing to my feet. "Isabeau." She didn't blink, didn't look at me, didn't respond to her name. "Isabeau." She'd told me to say it three times to pull her back into her body. I didn't know if it worked when I wasn't exactly in my body either. "Isabeau."

Nope. Didn't work.

She stayed ethereal and still, like she'd swallowed the moon. I felt tired and disoriented.

"Isabeau, damn it."

She turned her face slowly toward me. "Logan."

"Shit. You scared me," I grumbled, feeling drunk. My aura looked wrong, faded.

"You should get back into your body," she said urgently. "Right now."

"Good idea." I smiled sluggishly. "Isabeau?"

"*Oui?*"

"How exactly do I do that, *ma belle?*" French classes had been a good idea after all, and not just because Madame Veronique demanded a rudimentary understanding. I could charm Isabeau in her native tongue. She smiled at me. I was sure I hadn't imagined it. Well, pretty sure.

"Just sit back into it, as if you were sitting in a chair."

"Okay." I touched her cheek, or tried to. Our auras touched, sparked. "You don't smile enough."

"Flirt with me later, Logan." She shoved me and I tumbled, falling backward and landing in my body. My arms and legs twitched, as if electricity coursed through me. I felt heavy and weird and tingled all over. Charlemagne nosed me roughly, leaving a wet cold smear on my neck. I sat up, grimacing. "Not the kiss I was hoping for, dog," I told him. He nudged me again and I froze. I'd heard it too that time. Footsteps, bodies moving with vampire speed between the trees.

Toward us.

Isabeau was lying too still, she wasn't back in her body yet.

Before they could spill into the clearing, I leaped into the air and landed in a crouch at her feet, stake in my hand. Charlemagne stood by her head.

He relaxed when the Hound warriors surrounded us.

I didn't.

Magda stepped forward, her face unreadable.

"Logan Drake, come with us."

"Like hell."

Isabeau still wasn't moving and I had to warn my parents, had to make sure Solange was safe.

"This is not a request." There were dogs at her feet, ears pricked, teeth bared.

I snarled. "Look, you're at the bottom of my list of priorities right now, Magda. Take a freaking number."

"You have been summoned by Kala."

"She can wait too."

Isabeau jerked once and then sat up abruptly. She blinked dazedly.

"Magda? What's going on?"

Magda tossed her long curls back over her shoulder. "He's been summoned for the rites."

"What?" Isabeau leaped to her feet, nearly knocking me onto my face. "No!"

I rose slowly. "What are you talking about?"

"It's not like that," Isabeau said pleadingly at the warriors.

"Kala read the bones again," one of them said. "He has to prove himself worthy of you, of the Hounds. He has to be strong enough to be one of us."

"You never told me," Magda added, sounding hurt.

Isabeau winced. "I know. But it doesn't mean he's the one. And anyway, we don't have time for this."

"You can't be handfasted without the rites," another warrior insisted. "He has to be initiated if he'd going to be your consort."

"Consort?" I echoed. I stared at her. "Consort? Seriously? That's what they meant?"

She blushed lightly. "One of our traditions," she said softly. She weaved on her feet, fatigue making dark bruises under her green eyes. "Kala predicted that I would promise myself to a vampire of the royal courts. To a Drake."

"And here I thought you didn't like me."

"It's not like that." She pushed her hair out of her face. "We have to warn the others," she said. "Kala's orders."

My fangs were out, my fists clenched. "Let me at least call my parents to warn them."

Isabeau looked crestfallen. "Phones won't work here, not after all the magic that's been done. It's why phones don't work in the caves either."

"Then send someone to somewhere where they do work," I ground out. I reached for her hands, remembered the thin girl stealing coins and eating stale crusts of bread, the woman I'd kissed just this morning as the sun rose like a candle set too close to lace curtains. "If I do this," I asked huskily, "I'm proving myself to you?"

She nodded almost shyly. "Yes, but—"

I cut her off, turning to the band of armed warriors.

"Let's go."

CHAPTER 18

Logan

The march back to the caves was formal and irritating. At least Magda wasn't smirking at me anymore. Isabeau was bewildered and embarrassed. I probably should have been more concerned about my own welfare, but I was kind of glad to have a chance to prove myself to her. Even if it was the worst possible timing. And I'd been tested before, by Madame Veronique, who might prefer embroidery to warfare but was still remarkably intimidating.

Possibly I was underestimating this test.

Most of the torches had been doused inside the caverns; only a few candles were left burning along the edge of the milky lake. Kala already looked better, sitting on a worn stone, her amulets and bone beads clacking together when she shifted. Warriors lined the walls with their dogs. I could only see the glint of their eyes.

The ground was swept clean of pebbles and broken chunks of sta-lactites but sprinkled with what looked like salt and dried herbs.

"Logan Drake, do you come to the rites willingly?" Kala asked me, her voice echoing in a way that wasn't entirely a result of the caves.

I stripped off my jacket and my shirt. "These things aren't cheap," I muttered, folding them on a ledge. Someone sneered. I could just imagine what they must think of me in my pirate-style frock coat and steel-toe boots. It was easy to assume a guy who was comfortable wearing lace cuffs might not know a sword from a toothpick. I was used to it. And I knew how to use it to my advantage.

Isabeau swallowed, sent me a look I couldn't quite decipher. She opened her mouth with a warning but the man next to her clapped his hand over her mouth. I scowled.

"You know the rules," Kala told her sharply. "The bones and the dreams are not to be ignored."

"I'll be fine," I assured her. I raised an eyebrow at the Hounds still muscling her into silence. "Get off her." I couldn't believe she was allowing it. These traditions must run deeper than I'd thought. "Now."

He smirked and let his hand drop but didn't move away from her. Charlemagne didn't look as if he felt the need to bite the man's face off so I supposed I shouldn't either. It probably didn't bode well that a dog had better self-control when it came to Isabeau than I did.

Kala shook a seed rattle hung with dog teeth. The sound was

like rain on a tin rooftop. Six other Hounds lifted their own rattles and joined the prayer. Kala was chanting in a language that sounded like Sanskrit accented with guttural Viking-esque sounds. If I closed my eyes I could have been in some beautiful desert temple . . . or about to be ripped apart by a Viking Beserker in bear armor.

The song ended, the rattles trailing off into silence.

"Begin," Kala barked.

I tensed, half expecting vampires to rush at me howling. Nothing happened. There was the cold silence of the caves, the steady drip of water into the lake, the shifting of dogs. The unremarkable quiet moment was nearly worse than an out-and-out attack. That at least I had some vague idea how to handle. This was unnerving.

It was meant to be.

I lifted my chin arrogantly, standing with loose knees, ready to spring. I could take what they threw at me. And hell if I'd let them see me squirm and sweat.

And then I heard it.

The growl was low enough that I nearly felt it rumble in the ground under my feet.

The dog was that big.

He had the heavy bulk of Ox-Eye, with a generous dash of Doberman and Rottweiler. Drool plopped into the dust as his lips lifted off teeth that would have done a *Hel-Blar* proud. It was all muscle, not an ounce of soft puppy fat anywhere. And he was trained to fight and kill, with a leather collar armed with spikes to protect him from his prey. I'd heard they'd used dogs like this in the gladiator rings in ancient Rome and to hunt boar in the Middle Ages.

Knowing that hardly gave me an advantage though; just a shot of adrenaline in my veins.

I should have known they'd use dogs. And if I hurt it, even to save my own skin, they'd likely kill me for it anyway. The other dogs ringed around us in the dark growled in response.

Trial or trick?

Too late to regret my rash decision now.

I knew better than to back away or make eye contact. And I didn't have a handy drugged slab of steak with which to distract it. Just my own pitiful self.

This whole tribal negotiation thing just sucked.

Not to mention crushing on a girl who came from a tribe of bloodthirsty lunatics.

The dog paced toward me, head lowered threateningly, stalking me.

I wasn't going down like a damned gazelle. That would hardly prove my worth to Isabeau.

Very possibly this was the night my white-knight complex, as Solange put it, would get me killed. Someone had better write a poem about it. It was only fair.

I held my ground. There was nowhere for me to go at any rate, I was surrounded by warriors and their dogs. The light glimmered off the silver buttons of my coat on the ledge. If I was very lucky, I might be able to flip up and land on the narrow stone outcrop and climb out of reach. I looked back at the slavering war dog and bent my knees further, waiting. Everything else receded: Isabeau's carefully blank expression, the telltale way she clutched her hands together, the flickering light, the thunder of the waterfall. It was just me and the dog and the uneven stone.

I had one chance.

I carefully made eye contact and bared my fangs.

He didn't waste a single moment on barking or growling. His legs bunched up and he lunged at me, all teeth and wild eyes. His collar gleamed viciously. I bent, pushed off, and flung myself into a backflip that would have done any acrobat proud. I sailed gracefully through the air, nearly grinning.

The landing, however, wiped my smirk right off. The steel toe of my boot jammed into the wall. There wasn't enough room for my entire foot, and not enough of a handhold to keep me comfortably upright. The stone crumbled under my heel as I teetered, cursing. I slipped, dropped to the ground. The jagged rock tore at my arms, drawing thick rivulets of blood. I nearly lost a tooth bashing the side of my face.

No one was looking at me anyway.

There was a snap of teeth on air and another growl. Charlemagne sailed out of his position at Isabeau's feet and landed between me and the war dog. He landed with more power and grace than I'd shown. He snapped his teeth, growling. The war dog paused, lowered his ears, and promptly sat down, whining.

My mouth dropped open.

Kala inclined her head. "Very good," she said.

I wiped blood and grime off my hands. "What the hell just happened?"

"You passed the first trial," she said as if I was slow, as if this sort of thing was perfectly normal. "And, much more impressively, one of our own dogs claimed you as his own. That does not often happen."

I blinked sweat out of my eyes. Charlemagne's tongue lolled happily out of his mouth.

Kala sprinkled a handful of dried herbs and what looked like chalk into a small fire burning at the limestone bank of the white lake. "Ground-up bones of some of our most sacred dogs," she explained. She pointed to the hundreds of grottolike shrines that had been dug into the rock. They each held a candle or clay urns. "We keep them all close by, along with the ashes of our Mothers." I assumed "Mother" was another term for "shamanka."

And the smoke from the fire filled my nostrils and I stopped caring about semantics and powdered bones. The Hounds seemed to fade slightly into the background and Isabeau might as well have had a spotlight on her. She glowed like pearls and stars and moonlight. She was even more beautiful than usual, her long straight hair gleaming, her stance graceful, nearly coquettish. She wore a slinky dress of clinging satin in a deep burgundy, slit up one leg practically to her hip. Her slender leg emerged as she took a step forward. My mouth went dry. She wasn't wearing any jewelry, only those faded scars.

And she was smiling at me.

"Logan," she said softly, her green eyes glowing with amusement and heat as she approached me.

"Isabeau," I croaked. My voice cracked in a way it hadn't done since I was thirteen years old. I felt about as suave as I had then.

The fire crackled beside us, sending out curtains of scented smoke that lingered in the air between us and the others. We might have been entirely alone in the caves, in the whole world even.

She stopped when she was close enough to lick me without leaning forward.

Which she did.

She kissed me so thoroughly the war dog could have snuck up behind me and chomped on my leg and I wouldn't have noticed. She tasted sweet, like mulled wine and spices. Her tongue touched mine and I pulled her so close against my chest there was no room between us even for the billowing smoke. She nipped at me playfully and then she was soft and pliant in my arms, clinging to me and sighing my name.

It took a moment for coherent thought to hit me.

Isabeau would never sigh and cling like that, never run her hand under my shirt, along the waistline of my trousers with her entire tribe watching.

Not Isabeau.

It still required a supreme application of will to enable me to pull away. She was barely an inch from me, our noses practically touched. She licked her lower lip. I lost my train of thought. *Shit, man up, Drake*, I told myself.

She nuzzled my ear until shivers touched my spine.

"Logan, let's leave this place," she murmured. "Leave the Hounds and the Drakes and all of the politics. It could be just you and me. Alone."

There was probably a really good reason why I shouldn't agree with her and let her lead me out of the caves. As soon as the blood returned to my brain, I'd remember what it was.

She nibbled on my earlobe and I knew I was in trouble. Serious trouble. Vampire megalomaniacs and civil wars had nothing on this girl.

"Come with me, Logan."

It was physically painful to pull away. The smoke seemed thicker, it clung to her hair and stuck in my throat.

She ran a silver awl needle across the delicate skin of her inner wrist. I could see the blue rivers of her veins. Warm fragrant blood pooled on her winter-cool skin, across her arm to drip on the ground. She held up her red wrist.

"Drink, Logan. I want you to."

Self-control around fresh blood was never exactly easy for a very young vampire. I knew if I hadn't drunk my fill earlier that evening I'd have been utterly lost. Isabeau and blood were just too much to resist when put together. As it was I had to clench my back molars, trying to stop my fangs from protruding. I was only half successful.

She smiled, licked a drop of blood from her fingertip.

"I'm offering, Logan."

I snarled when my fangs won the battle with my gums and clenched jaw. I grabbed her elbow and dragged her toward the lake.

She giggled.

Definitely not the real Isabeau.

The smoke followed us. Her blood trailed pink ribbons in the milky water.

"What are you doing?" she asked nervously. She shifted, bared her leg invitingly.

But I'd already remembered what she'd told me earlier, when we were in spirit form. The trio of fat candles flickering on my left sent just enough light skittering on the pearly surface of the lake. I jerked her a little closer, angling her so I could see her reflection.

The lake might not be an actual mirror, but it was close enough.

I saw the smoke in the vague shape of a woman. It was the first time I'd come this close to the old myth of vampires not having a reflection.

I let go of her with a stifled curse, jerking back so quickly I would have spun her off her feet if she'd been real. I was alone suddenly in the smoke, grinding my heel in the dirt as I turned to glare at the Hounds. They weren't standing in the shadows anymore.

Kala didn't smile but she looked faintly pleased. "Last test," she murmured.

"Which is what exactly?" I asked suspiciously.

"Trial by combat."

I nearly sighed. "Of course it is," I muttered, unsurprised. I might have been more worried if I hadn't been defending myself against six brothers my whole life. And if I didn't have a mother who thought she was a ninja.

"Morgan." Kala motioned a woman out of the crowd. She looked barely sixteen, wearing a gray velvet dress that fell to her bare feet. Her hair hung to her knees in three fat braids, all clattering with bone beads, some painted blue, some gold. She was graceful, dainty, small as a ballet dancer.

I wasn't fooled.

Especially when she leaped at me, without even a warning battle shriek—even the telltale sound of her sword scraping its scabbard as she pulled it free was nonexistent. I wasn't going to be able to dance my way out of this one. I went low, rolling under her feet before she landed. When I flipped back up into a standing position she was already spinning to face me.

I had to leap backward so the tip of her sword didn't take my nose right off. The bracelets around her wrist jingled prettily. Since I happened to like my face where it was, I turned into my lean and kicked out. I got her in the solar plexus but not with enough force to actually cause any damage. She'd anticipated me and was fast enough to avoid the full punch of my heel. She grabbed my boot as it passed and yanked hard. I fell back, smashing my elbow and shoulder into the uneven rock. The flames of the candles by my head trembled.

This was ritual to the Hounds; they didn't holler or clap, only chanted and shook the occasional rattle.

It was both annoying and creepy.

When she came at me again, I stuck out my leg and tried to trip her. She stumbled but didn't fall. It did give me enough of a pause to get back up though. I flicked my hair out of my eyes. Blood smeared over my back from the rocks, dripping down my arm. Double and triple sets of fangs extended all around me. Morgan's nostrils flared.

And then there was just no escaping her attack.

She jabbed at me like a hornet, her sword drawing blood at my wrist, arm, chest, thigh. I fought her off as long as I could, landing a few blows but nothing definitive enough to win me the fight. And then, somehow, I was sailing through the air. I landed at Isabeau's feet, her boot digging into my ribs.

So much for proving myself to her.

The tip of Morgan's sword, already stained with my blood, rested on my Adam's apple. I froze and tried not to swallow. It seemed to take forever before Morgan stepped back, sheathed her sword, and glided away. I swallowed convulsively. Isabeau crouched down, half smiling.

"That was brilliant."

It almost made my total humiliation bearable. I pushed up out of my sprawl. "Did you miss the part where she kicked my ass?"

She shrugged one shoulder. "Morgan always wins. She's our champion."

I frowned. "I don't get it."

"It wasn't about winning. Only two Hounds have beaten her in the last one hundred and fifty years."

"Then what the hell was it about?" I held up my hand. "You know what, never mind. I don't think I care."

Kala approached us. "Well done, Logan Drake. We now consider you a brother."

"Yeah? Cool."

She handed me my shirt and jacket, and a leather thong with a dog's tooth wrapped in copper wire. "This was one of Charlemagne's baby teeth. It marks you as one of us and has magic worked into it."

I slipped it over my head as the Hounds traded rattles for drums. The bruises around my right eye pulsed. "Thanks." The drumbeats echoed all around us and a fire was lit in the center of the cave.

"Ordinarily we would celebrate and dance until dawn." Kala lowered her voice. "But I understand you have matters to attend to?"

I nodded. "I'm sorry."

Isabeau turned to me. "Yes, we should go." She slanted me a glance as we climbed the rough-hewn steps to the balcony-type ledge. "Logan?"

"Yes?" I pulled my clothes back on even though the fabric stuck to my wounds. So much for trying to keep them clean.

"How did you know it wasn't really me?"

"Are you kidding? Your eyeballs could be on fire and you wouldn't bat your lashes at me like that."

CHAPTER 19

Logan

We reached the ledge when the barking started.

At first it sounded like it was coming from far away, echoing down the stone passageways. Once it reached the main cavern the other dogs joined the chorus, barking, growling, howling. The hairs on my arms stood up. The Hounds went on high alert instantly, reaching for weapons. I strained to hear beyond the dogs' frantic singing. Kala clapped her hands and spoke a one-word command, sharp as broken glass. I'd have shut up too if I were a dog. Hell, I'd have shut up anyway.

Isabeau tilted her head. I heard a faint thump, three long, one short, as if something was hitting a pipe. It clanged toward us, so shrill I thought the water of the lake might have rippled slightly.

"Attack," Isabeau said, mostly for my benefit. I expected

everyone else there knew exactly what those series of sounds had meant. All I wanted was to get out and warn my family about Montmartre's attack. "A warning for battle and—" She stopped, clearly stunned to hear two more short clangs. "And to hide," she elaborated finally, as if such a thing had never occurred to any of them before.

I hated to think what could make the entire pack of Hounds, on their own territory and with their war dogs, blanch.

I wasn't eager to hang around and find out.

Discretion was definitely the better part of valor sometimes— plus, someone had to save Isabeau from herself.

I knew for a fact that she would jump into the fray, regardless of the danger. I was frankly amazed she hadn't gotten herself killed already.

Morgan was standing guard over Kala, ushering the shamanka toward a narrow crevice in one of the far walls, hung with cobwebs. Most of the dogs went with them. Isabeau snapped her fingers and pointed for Charlemagne to join them. A few of the more ferocious ones stayed behind with the Hounds. The efficient way they stepped into battle formation would have brought tears of joy to my mother's eyes.

A shriek echoed toward us. I whipped one of my daggers into my hand. Isabeau lifted her sword grimly. I heard scuffling, grunting, and then a Hound trailing blood from a head wound stumbled onto the ledge. I nearly skewered him. The fact that he collapsed at my feet saved his life and the future of the alliance between our tribes.

"*Hel-Blar*," he gurgled, choking. "Dozens of them."

"Shit," I said as Isabeau and I stared at each other wide-eyed. I went cold all over. "It's misdirection."

"What do you mean?" she asked as Hounds scrambled up to wait on either side of the tunnel. Someone dragged their wounded compatriot out of the way so he wouldn't be trampled once the fighting began.

"It's Montmartre," I said. "It has to be. He wants to discredit our tribes to each other to make sure none of you come to our aid." I went even colder, if that was possible. I wouldn't have been entirely surprised if ice had formed in my mouth. "He's going for the royal courts tonight," I said. "Now. They've moved up the attack and this is how he's going to keep the Hounds out of the way."

Her hands curled into fists. "Greyhaven might have sensed me at Montmartre's. He would know my spirit signature. He'd have reacted accordingly."

"I have to get out. I have to get to my family."

She nodded. "I know."

"Show me the nearest passageway."

"This way." She led me to the other side of the water and shimmied down a rope, swinging onto another ledge behind the curtain of white water. When the thick rope swung back, I grabbed it and followed her. The ledge was slippery and the thunder of the waterfall shook through my bones. Isabeau fumbled for a flashlight and switched it on, sending the beam bouncing down a tunnel that was really no more than a crack in the rock.

"Parts of it are so dark not even we can see," she explained, handing me another flashlight with a strap to fit it over my head.

She was fitting her own, like a headband. The light blinded me from seeing her expression. "You shouldn't go alone," she said. The clash of swords floated down, barely audible.

I stared at her briefly. "You're coming with me?" I hadn't expected that, wouldn't have imagined for a single moment that she'd leave the Hounds to help me. She turned away to face the passageway, light swinging.

"I expect I'll do more good with you than I would here. Kala didn't ask me to join her, which means she wants me to safeguard the alliance. Why else would she have insisted on your initiation so soon after meeting you?"

I didn't really have time to talk her out of it. "Thank you," I murmured as we wedged ourselves into the damp tunnel, rock scraping each of my shoulders. I turned sideways. There was still barely room to maneuver. I really hoped this crevice led in the right direction. They all looked the same from the outside. I really didn't relish the thought of getting stuck and starving to death inside a mountain. Hardly an effective way to stop Montmartre.

We crept along slowly, too slowly for both our tastes but there wasn't anything we could do about it. There was no way to move faster since the tunnel seemed to be getting even more narrow instead of widening up to the sky.

"I hope you know what you're doing," I muttered as I scraped another layer of skin off the side of my neck and the back of my hand. The flashlight speared Isabeau's back, the fall of her dark hair, pale glimpses of skin. She turned her head slightly, reached up to flick the light off.

"We're nearly there. If we keep these on we'll give ourselves away."

I shut mine off as well. After a moment of blinking away the sudden change in light I could differentiate all the shades of black and gray. If I'd still been human, it would have been unrelieved pitch-black. I could smell a change in the air too. It was still cold and damp but every so often a warm breath of leaves and mud snuck its way in. It wasn't long before I could hear the wind.

We stumbled out into a very small cave that opened up to the glimmer of stars and the shifting of branches from a stunted tree near the opening. The outcrop was relatively narrow, we'd have to climb our way down. I reached for my cell phone.

"I should call my parents. Can I get reception here?"

Isabeau nodded. "You should be able to. It's not reliable but at least it shouldn't be blocked by magic this far away from the main cavern."

The faceplate of my phone was cracked and it wouldn't turn on at all. "That just figures," I said, frustrated. "I wasn't sure I believed in magic before, but I totally believe in curses now." I stuffed it back into my pocket, disgusted. "I must have landed on it when Morgan was kicking my ass. It's useless." Kind of like I was starting to be. It was doing nothing for my mood.

Isabeau handed me her phone. "Here, try mine."

"Thanks." I dialed quickly, listening with growing agitation as it rang and rang. I tried my mother's number, my dad's, Sebastian's. No one answered. That was virtually unheard of unless they were hunting or fighting. Someone always answered. "This is not good," I said, dialing the farmhouse.

Solange answered on the second ring. "Hello?"

"Sol? What's going on? Why isn't anyone answering their phones?"

There was a long pause and when she spoke again her voice squeaked. "Logan?"

"Yeah, who else?" I answered, irritated.

"Logan!" she shouted so loudly and suddenly I nearly dropped the phone.

"What are you yelling for? And, ouch." Isabeau looked at me questioningly and I shrugged. I couldn't explain my family at the best of times.

"You're alive! Oh my God."

"Of course I'm—"

"Nicholas! It's Logan. He's okay. I don't kn—hey, you're such a pain in my—stop it!"

They were clearly fighting over the phone. Solange won. I could hear Nicholas shouting: "You kicked me!"

"Oh, Logan, I am so happy to hear your voice." Her own voice wobbled a little, as if she were crying.

"Hey," I said. "I'm okay. Don't cry, Sol. I'm fine."

"Okay." She sniffled once. "Where the hell have you been?"

I had to angle the phone away from my ear again when she got shrill. "I'm at the caves with Isabeau. I told one of the guards to let you know. Jen came with me . . ." I paused. "She didn't make it."

"What happened?"

"We got attacked by *Hel-Blar*. Kind of like we are right now, so I can't exactly chat."

"Logan, everyone thinks you're dead. That guard never told us anything except that he found a death charm with your scent on it and Isabeau's mark. Dad's been trying to stop Mom from attacking the Hounds. Finn's been calming her down."

"Shit. Listen, I really can't talk. Montmartre has been setting the *Hel-Blar* on all of us. It's misdirection. He wants us to fight among ourselves so we can't fight him. He's probably at the courts right now. Can you get hold of Kieran? If neither Mom or Dad are answering their phones we're going to need help. And fast."

"I'll call him now."

"Good. Tell him I'll meet him there."

"You'll meet us all there."

"Stay home, Solange. I mean it."

"I'm glad you're alive but bite me, Logan. I mean it."

"Montmartre wants *you*."

"Duh. But if misdirection has worked so well for him, we can make it work for us too."

"I'm not using my baby sister as bait. Not after what happened on your birthday. He almost had you, Sol. If it hadn't been for Isabeau and the Hounds . . ."

"See you soon. Bye, Logan."

"Wait, you can't—argh! She hung up on me. Brat."

"You can't expect her to sit at home when her family is being threatened."

I glanced at Isabeau thoughtfully. "Maybe you could go sit with her. Protect her."

She snorted. "You're very transparent, Logan."

"Please?"

"Non. Absolument pas."

I would have argued a great deal longer if something heavy hadn't struck the side of my head, sending me teetering on the edge of the outcrop. I stumbled back, blood dripping into my eyes. Pain lanced through my skull. Isabeau whirled, sword in hand, but we were too late. *Hel-Blar* dropped down from the cliffside above us and others climbed up from below. Their skin was an odd shade of blue in the darkness, their teeth like bone needles. The stench of rot was suddenly overpowering. Isabeau gagged, swore in French.

We fought like cats suddenly dunked in cold water. There was virtually no thought, it was instinct and a feral need to survive. I wasn't moving as quickly as I should have been. The head wound was tripping me up, making my arms feel uncoordinated and heavy. I kicked out, threw a stake with poor aim but enough anger to cata-pult the *Hel-Blar* off the side of the mountain. Isabeau pressed her back to mine, cutting off a blue arm, a blue hand.

"We're outnumbered," I slurred. "And I'm wounded. Run."

"You're not a white knight and I'm not a damsel in distress."

She was so stubborn I hissed. "Look around, Isabeau. This def-initely qualifies as distress. Now, run, damn it. I'm only holding you back."

"Shut up and fight, Logan."

Every girl I knew was entirely insane.

Unfortunately, Isabeau probably couldn't have **run even if she'd** agreed to it. The only escape was launching ourselves right off the cliff and we'd need to get past three salivating *Hel-Blar* to do even that. My head felt like a rotten pumpkin, oozing and not entirely containable in its casing. We managed to take out one of the *Hel-Blar* and he puffed into mushroom-colored ash, but his demise only served to enrage his already unstable companions.

I stumbled, dizzy, and when I fell to one knee, another rock came down on my head. There was a burst of fire and shooting stars and then nothing.

I didn't know how long I'd been unconscious.

It couldn't have been a full day, since my head still throbbed, though at least it didn't feel torn open. The scratches and gouges and bruises had all faded. My hands and feet tingled, mostly because they were locked in place with chains. I pulled and yanked. They rattled alarmingly but didn't budge.

"Isabeau," I hissed. "Isabeau!"

"I'm here," she said. "Behind you."

Her voice had relief flooding my system like champagne. I could've gotten drunk on the feeling.

"Thank God. Are you hurt?" I tried to turn, couldn't quite manage it from where I was lashed to the chair. Fury and pain replaced the relief and had me tensing every muscle until my jaw threatened to pop. I tested the chains again.

"It's no use, Logan," she said softly. "I've tried."

If I turned slightly I could see the side of her face and neck in a heavy mirror hanging on the wall beside us. There were bruises on her throat and over her cheekbone. We were in a small room with chains on the wall and several heavy wooden chairs. A window was hung with a thick curtain but I had no doubt it was regular glass, not enough to keep sunlight from weakening us. I was young enough that if they left me in the sun for a few hours, I'd pass out and let them stake me without a single twitch of a fight. I kicked at the floor with my boot, disgusted. Then I frowned.

"Since when do *Hel-Blar* have Persian rugs? Or leave their victims unbitten?"

"They don't."

I stared at her reflection in horror. "Are you telling me one of them bit you?" Adrenaline jerked through me. A *Hel-Blar* kiss could turn even an ancient vampire. Their blood infected our own and made us as mad and vicious as they were.

"No," Isabeau assured me before I lost my cool completely. "I'm only saying that Montmartre has better control of them then we'd thought."

"Hypnos," I muttered. "Bet you anything it's because of that damned drug."

She shivered.

"I won't let them take you." Big words from a guy covered in his own dried blood. I must be ridiculous to her. I'd failed her, damn it. I should've been able to protect her.

"Montmartre never leaves a Hound unmarked. We're proof that he's not infallible, that he can't control everything. He fears us and tells himself that fear is hate."

"We've stopped him before. We'll stop him again. For good this time." Hell if I was going to let him run around threatening the people I loved for the next hundred years.

"Noble words," an amused voice interrupted us from the doorway. I didn't recognize him but I saw all the blood drain from

Isabeau's face, saw an almost animal-like pain twist her features. For a moment she looked like the young girl I'd seen struggling to survive in the alleys of the Great Terror. That fear was brief, quickly covered by a burning thirst for vengeance.

Which could only mean one thing.

It wasn't Montmartre after all.

It was Greyhaven.

CHAPTER 20

London, 1794

It took Isabeau nearly a year to save, steal, and weasel enough money to buy passage to England. Even then, she hardly knew what she was going to do when she set foot in London. She had her uncle's name, her father's assurance that he was selfish and arrogant, and two pennies left to her name. Cerise had refused to accompany her on the grounds that England was full of the English.

And the London docks were unlike anything she'd ever seen before. London was unlike anything she'd ever seen before, far removed from the familiar alleys of Paris. It was gray and blue and black, soot stained and stirring under a fog of indeterminate color that made her cough.

"You'll get used to it soon enough, lad," the old man she'd sat beside for most of the journey cackled at her, jabbing his bony elbow into her ribs. Even though she'd kept her disguise as a boy, she'd thought it prudent not to appear to be traveling alone, even if she hardly expected an old man with rotting teeth to protect her. Sometimes, it was the illusion that counted.

But now that she stood on the wharf, being jostled by surly merchants and sailors eager for the nearest pub and prostitute, she felt more uncertain than she thought. She'd been saving up for this moment for so long, had held it up as torchlight in the dark nights to see her through.

The reality was somewhat daunting.

Wagons trundled by, children in dirty, torn clothes waded into the mud of the Thames for abandoned goods that might fetch a pretty price streetside. Voices and horse hooves and smoke from countless chimneys made a soup of sound and smell that had her holding her nose.

"Do you know where society lives?" she asked her elderly companion.

"Lookin' for the fancy, are you? They don't take kindly to urchins and pickpockets, my lad."

"I wasn't—"

He harrumphed. "I was young once, my boy. No need to worry I'll give you away." He nodded to the west end of the sprawling city. "Mayfair is where polite society resides and best of luck to you."

"Thank you." She handed him one of her pennies. He bit into it to check its worth and then slipped it into his pocket with more nimble fingers than she might have given him credit for. They were gnarled and bent but fast all the same.

"Mind the watchmen, lad," he said in parting before tottering away. He paused long enough to make eyes at a buxom fishwife with a stained apron. She laughed and went back to shouting about mackerel and eel.

Isabeau huddled into her jacket and lifted her chin determinedly. If you looked like prey, the world treated you as such. She walked easily and confidently, strolling westward as if she knew exactly where she was going, as if she'd lived here all her life. No one had to know that her heart was thundering so quickly she felt ill and the muscles in the back of her neck were so tight she'd have a splitting headache by nightfall. All they had to see was a young boy with a quick step and a clever eye who was able to take care of himself.

She walked for a couple of hours, trying to count right and left turns so she wouldn't be hopelessly lost. There were girls with baskets of violets and oranges for sale, muffins and baked potatoes and shops with towers of candies decorated with powdered sugar, hats with plumes dyed yellow and pink and green, ribbons of every description, lemon ices, books, anything anyone could ever conceive of buying was available. There were no scorched stones or broken windows from riots, no smell of fires or radicals shouting on every corner. It was utterly alien, decadent, and soft. But she couldn't afford to let her guard down just yet, if ever.

She began to notice the state of carriages improving; the streets were cleaner with boys waiting with brooms to clear a path through the horse droppings for a coin. The houses grew larger, the smells less pungent. Trees clustered in back gardens. When she came across the huge park, she stopped abruptly. She'd missed lawns of grass and thick oak trees and flowers everywhere. She hadn't realized how much she'd missed it until now. At least she knew where she would sleep tonight if she couldn't find her uncle. The thought bolstered her.

"Here now, mind yourself," a gentleman snapped, nearly walking into her immobile form. She snapped her jaw shut. She ducked her face into the shadows under the brim of her cap and stepped aside to let him pass.

She tore her gaze away from the horses and their well-clad riders picking their way into the park and followed the ornate carriages that trundled past. A vast majority of them were headed in the same direction and she took that as a good sign. It was still early morning; they wouldn't be off to balls and parties or shopping for new gowns. She didn't think the English aristocracy was that different from the French; mornings were for long breakfasts, correspondence, and resting after the excesses of the night before. More than a few of the carriage occupants were probably on their way home and hadn't even been to bed yet.

The houses became palatial, with gleaming brass door knockers and giant urns overflowing with every kind of flower. Maids walked small pet dogs on leashes and the occasional cat. Delivery boys, fish carts, and muffin sellers made their way to and from back doors. She stopped a rag man.

"St. Croix house?" she asked in halting English.

"Eh, Frenchie? Speak up?" He cupped his hand to his ear, barely stopping as he pulled his cart past. She helped him maneuver it over a protruding cobblestone.

"St. Croix?" she repeated.

"You mean St. Cross? House at the end of the street with the blue door." He waved in its direction and continued on his way without a backward glance. Her heart started to race again. Part of her wanted to run toward it, another part briefly considered running in the opposite direction. She would never let that part win. She forced herself to pick up her pace, though she did pause at the end of the walkway to catch her breath.

The townhouse loomed over her, several stories high, with a freshly painted blue door and brocade curtains in every window. Carriages rumbled behind her. An oak sapling dropped acorns on the street and sidewalk. Roses bloomed in copper urns. A lane led along the house to the back, where the gardens and stables and servant entrances were located.

She climbed the steps, which were swept clean of even a single petal. The door knocker was in the shape of a lion with a cross in its mouth. Isabeau ran her fingers over her family crest before letting it fall with a thud against the door. It swung open and a man with thick gray hair looked down his nose at her. His black jacket was perfectly pressed, his cravat immaculate.

"*Oncle* Olivier?" she asked tentatively. She'd never met him before but she'd expected he'd have some family resemblance, her father's cheekbones perhaps, or the famous St. Croix green eyes. This man was taller than any of her relatives and sniffed disdainfully.

"Lord St. Cross does not receive muddy boys who smell like you do," he informed her. "Off with you." He went to shut the door. She shoved her foot against it.

"Attend, s'il te plaît!" Her cap dislodged in her agitation, letting her hair spill out. She knew she must look half wild with her babbling in another language and her pleading, watery eyes. *"Non! Monsieur!"*

"If you go to the back door Cook will feed you, child. And then on your way." He shoved the door shut. She yanked at the handle but it was locked. She bit back tears of frustration. Weeping wasn't going to help her. She'd just have to find another way in.

The butler had pointed to the lane along the house. She tromped along it, gathering mud on her boots. A light rain began to fall, further muddying the lane. One of the windows was partially open, the curtains billowing in the wind. She looked around to make sure no one was watching her before diving into the rosebushes to get a better look. Thorns scraped the back of her hands and pulled at her hair. Stupid roses. Petals fell over her, cloying as perfume under the warm rain.

The parlor had several chairs with embroidered cushions and a pianoforte in one corner. The ceiling was painted with cherubs. She shuddered. How was a person supposed to relax with fat floating babies staring at the top of her head all day long? Between the angels and the gilded candlesticks and shell-encrusted lamps, the room was hideously overly decorated.

But at least it was empty.

She pushed the window open a little more and then shoved her leg through the opening, hugging the sill as she squirmed her way inside. She could smell lemon wax and more roses. The house was remarkably quiet for one so large. She wondered if she had any cousins banished to the attic nursery. No dog came to greet her, no cat slunk out from under the table. Her heart resumed its regular pace.

She went out into the hallway, wondering where her uncle might be. If he was awake he'd surely be in his study. That was where her father had spent most of his time when he wasn't on horseback or escorting her mother to some soiree. Even the hall was beautiful, with framed paintings, gilded sconces, marble-topped tables, and urns of flowers. She had to fight the urge to slip a small silver snuffbox into her pocket.

She turned a corner and walked straight into the butler.

He yelped but was much faster than she'd anticipated and hauled her off her feet by the sleeve of her coat before she could dart out of his reach. Her instinct was to run and hide but that was hardly going to get her what she wanted. The butler shook her.

"I'm calling the magistrate. We don't take kindly to intruders here in England. I don't care if you are a girl!"

Isabeau did the only thing she could think of.

She opened her mouth and screamed at the top of her lungs.

"Mon oncle! Mon oncle!"

The butler recoiled at her impressive volume. The chandelier overhead rattled. Footmen came thundering toward them. A door burst open, slamming into the wall.

"What the devil is going on here?" The voice had only the faintest traces of a French accent. The man wore a gray silk waistcoat straining subtly over his belly. His graying hair was swept off his high forehead.

"I beg your pardon, your lordship," the butler wheezed. "I caught an intruder."

"*Mais non, arrête.*" Isabeau struggled to get out of his grasp. She blew her hair out of her face. "It's me," she said. "Isabeau St. Croix. Your niece."

"My niece?" he echoed in English.

Silence circled around them, thick as smoke. Her uncle blinked at her. The butler blinked at her uncle. The footmen blinked at all of them. A woman she assumed to be her aunt made a strangled gasp from another doorway. She wore a lace cap and a morning dress trimmed with silk ribbon rosettes.

"Your lordship?" The butler was no longer sure if he was apprehending a criminal or hauling an earl's niece about by the scruff of the neck.

"Let her go," Lord St. Cross said. "Let me get a look at her."

Isabeau straightened her rumpled and stained coat. Her uncle stared at her for another long moment before he clapped his hands together.

"By God, it is her!"

"Are you certain?" his wife asked, her fingers fluttering at her throat. "You've never met her."

"I haven't, but I'd know those eyes anywhere. Just like Jean-Paul." He shook his head. "Remarkable. Where is he?"

Isabeau swallowed. "He's dead."

Olivier's mouth trembled in shock. He went pale as butter. "*Non,*" he slipped into French. "How?"

"Guillotine."

His wife fanned herself furiously.

"And your mother?" he asked quietly.

"Same." She swallowed hard. She couldn't lose her composure now. She'd fought too hard for her father's sake to be the strong girl who survived. Her uncle's warm palm settled on her shoulder.

"Oh, my dear child."

His wife lowered her hands from where they'd been trembling at her mouth. "My Lord, look at her, she's terribly thin."

"You are rather scrawny, my girl. We'll send for tea. Bring extra biscuits," he told the nearest footman. "Our cook is French. We'll have him make your favorite for supper."

"Come by the fire," his wife urged kindly, leading her into the parlor. "I'll ring for a bath after your tea."

Isabeau followed, slightly dazed. She'd expected more of a fight. She felt off center, thin as dandelion fluff. She was shown to a deep comfortable chair by the hearth. The fire snapped cheerfully. Warmth made her cheeks red, her eyelids heavy. It was a far cry from the fires in the metal bins on street corners, or the flames from piles of broken wooden furniture used as barricades.

"She's in shock, I think," her uncle murmured. He shook his head. "Poor Jean-Paul."

"Oh, those terrible French."

"Careful, love. You married one," he teased her.

"Don't be ridiculous. You barely even have an accent anymore. Only a fondness for that awful pâté."

Isabeau pinched her leg to keep from dozing off. "Father was planning to bring us here. Before we were caught."

"Don't worry, my dear, we'll take care of you."

"You are nothing like he said," she blurted out, bewildered.

He chuckled. "No, I imagine not. We never did see each other plainly, even as children." He sighed. "Lady St. Cross and I weren't able to have a family of our own."

"Oliver, really," Lady St. Cross murmured, flushing. "What a thing to say."

He patted her knee, his arm big enough to knock her over, but she just smiled at him. He turned to Isabeau. "What I mean is, it will be nice to have a young lady in the house."

"Oh yes," Lady St. Cross exclaimed. "We'll take you to all the balls, my dear. We'll need gowns, of course, and the dancing master, a lady's maid to do your hair." Her eyes shone with enthusiasm. Isabeau wasn't sure whether she should be nervous.

"Don't fret," her uncle said jovially when Lady St. Cross was distracted by the arrival of the tea cart. "You survived the Terror, you'll survive being a debutante."

CHAPTER 21

Isabeau

Greyhaven.

The last time I'd seen him was at the Christmas ball, his frock coat immaculate, his smile charming. I had no experience with men like him, had given in to the magic of the night and one glass too many of champagne. I thought I'd seen all sorts of monsters in my eighteen years: prisoners, rebels, cruel power-hungry guards, pimps, and earls with too much money.

But how did you defend yourself against a monster you had never imagined could actually exist?

He'd tainted my first real moments of comfort, of trusting the first happiness I felt since the mob had stormed my family château.

I wanted to kill him all over again.

I struggled against my restraints, heedless of the raw gashes I was digging into my skin, of my blood smearing the iron manacles. Logan was saying something but I couldn't understand him over the roar in my ears. It was as if my head was being held underwater.

Greyhaven sounded just as cultured and smooth as he had two hundred years ago. The scars on my arms ached. "One of the Drake princelings," he said pleasantly to Logan. Logan didn't reply. "Rumor has it our girl here has murdered you."

Logan sneered. "Are you going to fix that oversight?" He didn't sound afraid, only faintly bored.

I was starting to be able to concentrate again. Blood pooled in my hands. My fangs stung my gums, hyperextended.

"Certainly not. You're worth far more to me as a hostage. These little revolutions aren't easy to bankroll, you understand."

"I'll pay double what you get for me if you let Isabeau go right now."

Greyhaven laughed. "You're eighteen years old, Logan, and hardly a self-made billionaire. You can't afford her, even were I inclined to give her up."

Logan yanked at his chains. If he pulled any harder, he'd dislocate his own shoulder.

"Logan, don't," I said. My voice was dry, as if I hadn't spoken in years.

"Ah." Greyhaven turned toward me. I tried not to move, not to flinch, or to lean closer snapping my fangs. If I reacted now, it would only give him pleasure.

And he would never get a single moment of pleasure from me.

"Isabeau St. Croix," he said, "you've certainly caused me no end of trouble."

I hadn't seen him since that night in my uncle's garden. I had no idea what he meant by that.

"What does Montmartre want with me?" I asked, even though I knew the answer. The same thing I wanted with Greyhaven: revenge. I'd foiled his plans to kidnap Solange Drake and had taken down his Host. And I was a Hound, something that was an affront to his sense of power and entitlement.

Even if he killed me—again—I wouldn't be sorry for it.

Greyhaven folded his arms, leaning negligently against the wallpaper, as if we were still at that ball. "This isn't about Montmartre, it's about you."

"What? He isn't attacking the courts?" Logan asked.

"Yes." Greyhaven smiled. "He is. And probably wondering where I am. But I just had to stop in to see you." He approached me slowly. I lifted my chin defiantly. "I had to know if you remembered me."

"Hard to forget my murderer," I spat. "You left me in that coffin for two hundred years."

"Yes, regrettable. If I had any idea just how strong you were, I'd have made more of an effort to retrieve you." He flicked a dismissive glance at my leather tunic and tall boots. "Though you dressed much better in 1795."

I snarled. "Why did you bring me here? Just to amuse yourself?"

Greyhaven shook his head sorrowfully. "It would have been

better if you hadn't remembered me. Now it's messy, and I can't abide a mess. I never could."

I was confused. All my dreams of finding Greyhaven involved my driving a stake through his gray, withered heart, not partaking in annoying chatter.

"You did all this just to test my memory?" I asked, perplexed. "The ribbon from my mother's dress," I added slowly. "The painting in the courts, the wine bottle. *That's* why?"

"Indeed."

"Not Montmartre?"

"He ordered the traps, certainly. He's not fond of you. But I did the work, as usual," he emphasized. "So why not use it to my own purpose?"

"You're stalking her, you git?" Logan, snorted, disgusted. I knew what he was trying to do. He wanted to make Greyhaven angry enough to take his focus off me. "Pathetic, don't you think? Especially for the Host."

His lips lifted off his face but he didn't look away from me.

He had more control than Logan gave him credit for.

Not especially heartening, actually.

At any rate, I wouldn't beg for Logan's life. Greyhaven was perverse enough to kill him just to watch me suffer. Better that Logan was worth something to his greed.

"This isn't easy for me, you know," he said conversationally, nearly apologetically. "You were my first. I consider myself your father."

"I had a father." I hissed through my teeth, every word like a flung dagger. "You're not him."

He waved that away. "I gave you life eternal."

"You gave me death."

"Semantics."

A red haze filled my eyes. Anger soaked through me like a monsoon. I tasted blood in my mouth from where I bit my tongue.

"I can't have you giving me away," he continued, sliding a lacquered black stake out of the inside pocket of his pinstriped jacket.

"Get away from her!" Logan shouted, chains rattling frantically. "Me for her! Me for her, damn it!"

I felt nearly mesmerized by Greyhaven's version of our story, as if he were talking about someone else. Emotional shock. I'd felt like this the first night in my uncle's house, touching the books, the thick blankets, eating too much at supper. Like everything was finally right, but nothing made sense. I felt removed.

But I could still hear him, could watch dispassionately as he approached, nearly close enough to kick; but not quite yet.

"I've taken great pains, planned, and been patient for over a century now. When I first joined, the Host was strong, organized, powerful. I climbed the ranks, paid my dues. And still Montmartre denies me my own fledglings. As if he could stop me forever. I deserve my own army, my own Host."

"How many have you done this to?" Logan demanded, horrified, as he realized what Greyhaven was really saying. "You're making *Hel-Blar*."

"I admit I tried. But *Hel-Blar* are weak castoffs and mistakes. Now I've chosen better. I'm smart enough not to repeat Montmartre's mistakes."

"Smart? Is that what we're calling it now?"

"You bore me, little boy. And you won't sway me with temper. But if you don't stop your childish tantrums, I'll gag you." He flicked the stake at Logan and it bit through his sleeve at his shoulder, pinning him to his chair.

"Now where were we?" Greyhaven still hadn't actually looked away from me, not for a moment. I might have shivered if I wasn't floating inside my own head, bewildered by memories and fury. "I'm sorry I didn't come back for you, Isabeau. Forgive me?"

That startled me out of my daze. He had to be joking. My answer was a string of curse words I'd learned from Cerise. The air should have blistered.

"I just can't have you giving me away. Not when I'm so close. If Montmartre finds out before I'm fully prepared . . ." He trailed off with a delicate shudder. "Well, as I said, I prefer things to be neat and tidy. The battle will be on my terms and the Host my own to command." He withdrew another stake, pointed at me. "You can say your prayers, if you like. You *were* always my favorite. You never forget your first."

When he was close enough that I could smell his expensive cologne and see the grain in the lacquered wood of his stake, Logan managed to hook his foot around the rung of the stool next to him. He jerked his foot with an audible snap and the stool whipped over his head. It caught Greyhaven in the back of his knees. He stumbled, fury making his face bone-pale. A small wooden disk engraved with a rose and three daggers fell out of his pocket. Just like the one we'd found in the woods the night Solange received the love charm. He hadn't been lying then. He really did have his own men.

I kicked him as hard as I could.

Logan gave a wholly undignified whoop of joy. He sounded like a child opening presents on Christmas Eve. I kicked again. My only goal was to make it as difficult for Greyhaven as possible.

"I was prepared to offer you a quick, honorable death," he said. "But now you'll both suffer."

There was a stake in his hand again but before he could follow through on his promise, the door slammed opened on its hinges.

"Greyhaven, quit playing with your new pet. You're needed."

Greyhaven turned to slant the new arrival a seething glance. "Can't you see I'm busy, Lars?"

"This can wait," Lars assured him, his voice cool, quiet. "Montmartre can't. You'll give us all away because you can never delay yourself a little gratification. The battle's begun and his lieutenant is lecturing little girls. It doesn't look good."

Greyhaven tensed his jaw until it looked as if it might crack. Then he smiled at me. "Only a momentary reprieve, I assure you," he said darkly. "Watch the doors," he told the guards before storming out, the door slamming behind him and Lars.

"That was too damn close," Logan muttered. "This is our only chance. Sounds like most of the Host are at the courts." He stood up. The chains hung from the ceiling, not quite long enough for him to lower his arms. He tugged, then swung with his entire body weight. Nothing.

I stood as well, inspected the locks on my manacles. "I might be able to pick these," I said. "But I need a pin of some kind." I was going to start wearing hair pins again just as soon as I got out of here.

We searched the room: fireplace utensils, cushions, lamps, a stack of magazines. Nothing useful.

"Are you wearing a bra?" Logan asked suddenly.

I frowned at him. "What?"

"A bra," he repeated. "Are you wearing one?"

"Yes."

"Can you get it off?"

"I suppose so. But how is that going to help?"

"The underwire comes right out. You can use that."

I really was beginning to like him more than I ought to.

I tried to maneuver my hands behind my back. My muscles screamed after a few minutes. I was undead, not boneless.

"I can't reach," I said finally.

"Turn around. Let me try." He rolled his eyes at my expression. "I'm not trying to cop a feel before I die, though the idea has merit." He stretched, swore. "Can't reach either. Stand on the chair."

I climbed up onto the seat, trying not to feel ridiculous. His hands grazed my back.

"Hold still," he said as if he was concentrating harder than he'd ever concentrated in his entire life. His vampire pheromones were suddenly stronger, flooding the room with the smell of anise and incense. It had no effect on me, of course, but it smelled nice. He made quick work of the lacing on the back of my tunic, exposing my bare back. His fingertips were cool and gentle on my skin. He reached for the clasp, had it apart in seconds.

"You're rather good at that," I remarked dryly.

He pushed my tunic down over my shoulder to reach the strap. I felt warm suddenly, tingly. I had to remind myself we were locked up, chained, and about to be killed. I heard him swallow. And then his mouth was on the back of my neck. He pressed a hot kiss there, searing through me.

Then he stepped back abruptly.

"Can you reach it now?" he asked hoarsely.

I nodded mutely and didn't turn around. I couldn't look at him just yet. I knew my face was red; my fingers trembled. My knees felt soft as I climbed off the chair. I reached into the armhole of my sleeveless tunic and pulled the bra strap down and then did the same on the other side. A quick shimmy and the bra slid out, dangling from my hand. It was white lace, a gift from Magda. And for some reason having it out where Logan could see it like that made me blush harder.

I used my fangs to bite a hole into the fabric and then I slid the thin steel wire out of one of the cups. Logan was watching me intently, his cheekbones ruddy. I wasn't the only one blushing over a scrap of lace. Somehow that made me feel better.

I inserted the end of the wire into the lock of the manacle on my right wrist and jiggled it gently, tilting my head to better hear the scrape of metal on metal. When I heard the delicate, barely audible snick, I smiled faintly. Another twist and the manacle opened. I slid my hand out and repeated the procedure on the other lock.

"Sweet," he said. "You'll have to teach me that trick."

The guards were still quiet on the other side of the door, but we didn't have much time. I hurried over and picked the locks to free him as well.

"Are you coming?" Logan grabbed Greyhaven's discarded stake off the rug and then looked over his shoulder when I didn't move. "Are you okay?"

"I'm fine, Logan," I answered calmly.

"Well, I'm not," he muttered. "We have to get the hell out of here."

"He's not after you, you have nothing to worry about."

He sucked in his breath, to express emotion rather than for need of oxygen. When he spoke, his voice was a little husky. "I'm not worried about me."

I didn't know what to do with this concern, with the way he looked at me, as if I mattered. I needed to stay strong, focused, cold. I couldn't afford to let him get in my way. I was too close now. I spent too long waiting for my chance.

And when Greyhaven came back in to kill me properly, I'd have that chance.

I couldn't regret not having the opportunity to explore the connection I felt with Logan.

And I did feel it.

In a few short nights, he'd broken through some of my defenses, had made me long for things that were impossible.

He was a romantic, charming, and loving.

And convincing.

I knew if I said a single word about the way he made me feel he'd spare no quarter in convincing me that we had a chance. But his kind of life just didn't have room for someone like me, no matter what Kala's oracle bones had said. His family was civilized. I was proud to be a Hound, but there was no denying we were a different vampire breed: wild, primal, superstitious. Not to mention disdained and feared by the other vampires.

And though Logan had passed his tests, had been initiated as a Hound, I couldn't know yet if he truly understood what that meant.

Just like he couldn't know that making Greyhaven pay had been the only thing to see me through my first days as a vampire.

How was I supposed to give that up, now that it was within my grasp?

"I have to stay," I finally said tonelessly. "You should go though."

"Don't be stupid. I'm not leaving without you," he argued. "And if you don't come with me, my parents—hell, my entire family—could die. You know Montmartre and you know how to sneak into the court caves. I *need you, Isabeau.*"

"I can't," I said brokenly. "I have to kill Greyhaven. *I have to.*" He was asking too much from me.

"If you stay, you'll die. He'll kill *you.*"

"Probably."

"So, what—I'm supposed to let you commit suicide?"

"It has nothing to do with you, Logan."

"Coward," he raged at me, the charming young man vanishing. The predator in him, usually disguised in lace and old-fashioned clothes, broke free.

Instead of being afraid, I leaned in closer to him subconsciously.

"I can't," I whispered again, jerking back.

"You have to," he insisted hotly. "You're a survivor. I saw what you lived through, so you can damn well live through this too. Survive Greyhaven, Isabeau. Please."

"You don't understand."

"I get it. And it's stupid. Now, I'm getting out of here and I hope you'll choose to fight instead of giving up." His eyes flared with green fire. "The Isabeau I know wouldn't give up. Not now. Not when her tribe is out there fighting."

He was right.

Insufferable, but right.

"Your choice," he said finally.

CHAPTER 22

Isabeau

My choice was to stay and get my vengeance—and likely die.

Or fight and only possibly die.

Logan made it sound so simple.

"I've only known you three days," I said. "And you're asking me to choose you."

He speared me with a glance. "I'm not asking you to feel for me the way I feel for you. I'm just asking you to choose *you*. Not Greyhaven."

I wasn't as strong as I'd thought. Because part of me really wanted to stay. It was easier, tidier, and hurt less.

Tidier.

Greyhaven thought like that.

Not me.

But if I wasn't the girl who brought down Greyhaven, who was I? I'd built my new life, my new identity, on that one single goal. But this was a battle of a different sort, one I couldn't win with a sword or a magic charm. Otherwise he'd keep winning, without even realizing it. I'd survived him once, but I'd carried him around and let him hurt me over and over again. And that part was on me.

And it was the only part of this whole mess, of the emotions and needs bubbling inside the cauldron of my chest, that I could control.

So I'd damn well control it.

"*Je viens*," I said tightly. When he looked at me blankly, I repeated myself in English. "I'm coming." Something broke inside and there was pain and sorrow and then, surprisingly, lightness. Ironically, it was as if I could breathe again.

Logan stepped close to me and slid his hand through my hair, cupping the back of my head, bone beads dangling against his fingers. He didn't kiss me but he looked at me with such a fiery kind of joy that I felt scalded all over.

And naked.

"Let's hurry," he said huskily. "So I can kiss you for an hour or two."

It was surprisingly good incentive.

"The window," I said as he stepped back. "It sounds as if most of the Host are busy with Montmartre. We couldn't ask for a better chance."

We quietly dragged a chair to the door and very carefully tilted it so it was shoved tight between the handle and the floor. We moved with studied caution since the guards would have hearing as good as ours. When no one raised the alarm we carried a table and set it under the window, then climbed up on top. I could just reach it. Logan nudged me out of the way and stuck his head outside, looking right then left.

"Clear," he mouthed before hauling himself up and out. He stayed low in the grass, reaching down to pull me out. We lay side by side for a long moment, just listening. The night was innocuous, crickets and frogs and an owl somewhere in the forest. I looked up, noting the stars.

"We're east of the courts," I told him. "They'll have guards posted just inside the trees."

"Can we outrun them?"

"Maybe."

"We're mounting a rescue without weapons," he muttered. "They stripped us bare."

"I know." I was very aware of the empty scabbard strapped to my back and the bare loops on my belt. They'd even taken the dagger hidden in my boot.

"Are you ready?"

I nodded, smiling grimly. I had enough pent-up frustration that taking on Host guards seemed like a calming pastime. Nearly as good as a bubble bath.

We managed to crawl to the lilac hedge before we noticed anyone at all. The house was quiet, windows casting squares of yellow light on the lawns. There was a carriage house behind the main building but it was dark. We were pressed in the mud, waiting for the wind to shift the leaves. Moonlight caught the metal zipper on a Host vampire's jacket. He was leaning against a tree, bored. I reached up to snap off a branch of the lilac. It wasn't exactly a sophisticated weapon but it was marginally better than my bare hands.

Logan touched my wrist, jerked his head toward the backyard, where the pool wafted chlorine fumes to tickle our noses. I had to press my tongue to the roof of my mouth to stifle a sneeze. Two more guards came toward us, from behind the pool shed.

We froze, hunched in the roots. They turned right, following a flagstone path that curved away from us. We waited a little longer before easing out of the hedge, rolling to a circle of birch trees. It was the last bit of cover between us and the forest. The guard yawned, shifted against the maple, startling a bird asleep near enough to notice a predator shifting.

Logan picked up a large stone, hefted it in his hand.

"Ready?" he murmured in my ear so low it was more of a tickle than an actual sound. I nodded, shifting into a crouch. He tossed the stone low but far enough so that it dropped into the bushes to the left of the guard. The leaves rustled.

The guard leaped into action, hurling himself toward the sound. We threw ourselves into a run, heading into the edge of the woods on his far right while he was momentarily distracted.

He wasn't the problem.

A shout came from the house, closely followed by a bright spotlight suddenly swinging across the lawn, bright as sunlight. Every blade of grass stood in sharp relief, the peeling bark of the birches, the blue ripple of the pool water.

Us.

"Hell," Logan muttered, tugging my hand. "Run!"

My feet barely touched the ground. Judging by the voices, there weren't many Host left behind, as we'd thought.

But certainly enough to kill us.

I stopped, spinning around, splintered branch held high. Logan skidded in the dirt.

"Are you *smiling?*" he asked incredulously.

"Just a little bit."

"Okay, well, could you run and smile at the same time?" The guards thundered out of the house, racing through the gardens, toward the forest and the fields behind the carriage house.

"I'd rather fight."

"Yeah, I get that." He shoved me, forcing me into a backward stumble. "Let's run anyway."

"There!" someone yelled. "I see them."

Logan kept pushing me until I had to run or trip over my own feet. We leaped a fallen trunk, blossoming mushrooms and moss. Branches slapped at us, catching in my hair. Leaves rained down on us. We darted around trees, zigzagging to make our trail harder to follow. We ran, splitting up at a clearing and rejoining on the other side, further muddying our trail. A rabbit darted out of our way and then we were truly in the dark secret of the forest.

Safe.

I was perversely disappointed.

Logan shot me a knowing grin. "Cheer up. You can hack someone to bits soon enough." He shook his head when I brightened, heartened.

I was even more heartened when I heard a plaintive dog howl. I paused, the abrupt switch from all-out running to dead stop making me briefly dizzy. When Logan realized I was no longer keeping pace, he doubled back. I held up my hand before he could say anything, listening harder. The howl came again, trailing at the end.

I knew that howl.

Grinning and watery-eyed at the same time, I stuck my thumb and forefinger in my mouth and whistled. It pierced the forest, shrill enough to leave Logan wincing.

"My ears are bleeding. Thanks for that," he said. "And so much for stealthy."

"We left the Host miles back," I assured him, whistling again. A series of yips answered. And then barking from across the river. A different howl from the mountainside.

It wasn't long before Charlemagne came running at me from between the trees. He leaped on me, tongue lolling happily. He wiped it across my cheek, tail wagging furiously. He gave Logan a swipe in greeting and then leaned so joyfully against me, I staggered under his weight.

"Good boy." I scratched his ears, then ran a hand over his fur, searching for wounds. He was unmarked.

More dogs came at us from all directions until we were surrounded. Logan raised his eyebrows, impressed. There were six aside from Charlemagne, three of them massive, trained Rottweiler war dogs.

"Finally," Logan remarked. "We have weapons again. Except that one looks like it wants to chew on my leg."

"He probably does," I said cheerfully, snapping my fingers to get the dog's attention.

Logan led the pack to where he'd arranged to meet his brothers and sister. Dogs sniffed ahead of us, ran behind us, and ran along either side.

I felt more like myself than I had in a long time.

CHAPTER 23

Logan

Solange, Nicholas, Connor, and Quinn were waiting for us. Connor was pacing; Quinn was crouched in the ferns. He rose when he spotted us, and Solange came running. The dogs milled around our feet.

"Logan!" She hugged me so tightly I grunted, extricating myself after tugging affectionately on her hair.

"I'm fine, brat. *Oof*," I mumbled, tripping over one of the eager dogs.

"I told you the Drake boys are harder to kill than that." Quinn smirked and clapped me on the shoulder. Nicholas and Connor did the same. They turned to Isabeau cautiously.

"Isabeau," Solange said politely.

I bumped her with my shoulder. "She didn't murder me, as you can see, so chill out."

Solange looked a little sheepish. "Sorry."

"I understand," Isabeau said quietly. "Could I borrow someone's phone?"

Solange handed hers over and Isabeau dialed quickly. "Magda? Are you all right? Kala?"

I could hear Magda's reply. "Kala's fine. We set some of the dogs loose to find you."

"I know. We found each other. Did you get rid of the *Hel-Blar*?" Isabeau asked.

We eavesdropped without pretense.

"Yes, but only just," Magda replied. "And we haven't had a chance to go back to the caves and make sure none are nesting."

"Listen, Montmartre's making his move tonight, right now, against the Drakes. We have to stop him."

"Why?" Magda snapped. Isabeau glanced my way, wincing. "What do I care about the royal courts? And we have enough problems of our own tonight, if you hadn't noticed."

"Believe me, I noticed," Isabeau shot back. "And if you want to know why, it's because we're next."

"Fine," she grumbled.

"I'll keep you posted." Isabeau clicked off.

"Where's Lucy?" I asked the others.

"At the farmhouse," Nicholas said with grim satisfaction.

"How'd you manage that?"

"She's in a closet." Solange rolled her eyes.

I stared at Nicholas. "You locked your girlfriend in a closet? Smooth."

"She's going to eviscerate him," Quinn said cheerfully.

"Yeah, well, she'll be alive to do it," Nicholas said. "And that's all I care about right now."

"What about the others? Mom and Dad at the courts?"

Connor shook his head. "No, and they never made it home. It's nearly sunrise, so they must have gotten caught in between. Sebastian and Marcus are with them."

I checked my pocket watch. "They can't have been ambushed that long ago. They'll still be alive. They have to be." I looked at Solange. "Did you call Kieran?"

"Yeah, but the Helios-Ra can't help us."

"Why the hell not? What's the point of dating a hunter if you can't use him?"

"They've got their hands full," Connor explained. "*Hel-Blar* are close enough to town to cause a serious problem."

"Greyhaven," I said, disgusted.

"What does he have to do with it?"

"He's been making vamps on the sly," I answered. "I guarantee most of them went feral. The ones who didn't are helping him plan a coup to oust Montmartre, while the others are being used as misdirection."

"Shit," Quinn said. "Bastard."

"You have no idea." I looked at Isabeau, but her expression was carefully blank. "So now the problem is, how do we find Mom and Dad in time?"

"I can help with that," Isabeau said confidently, "but I need something of theirs. A piece of clothing would be ideal."

"Magic?"

She shook her head, half smiling. "Dogs."

"Oh. Right."

Solange and my brothers looked at one another and shook their heads. "We've got nothing on us and no time to go home and get it," Quinn said.

"Wait." Solange opened her pack. "I have something that belonged to Montmartre. It was left at the property line in the woods. We found it on the way here." She pulled out a slender, delicate silver crown, dripping with diamonds and rubies. She made a face. "He doesn't go for the subtle metaphor, does he?"

"He gave you a tiara?" I grimaced. "Tacky."

"I know, right?"

"It's perfect," Isabeau said, plucking it out of her hands. "Gwynn," she called over one of the hounds. He was huge, taller than Charlemagne with a distinctly regal bearing. He padded over to her and she held out the crown. "Scent," Isabeau demanded. Obediently, he sniffed the ornate filigrees, the egg-sized rubies and seed pearls. "Good boy. Now find Montmartre!"

He *woofed* once and fit his nose to the ground, smelling through the undergrowth. Isabeau made sure the other dogs received the same instructions, giving them a good thorough scent of the crown. "Find Montmartre!" she repeated.

"Your dogs have a 'find Montmartre' command?" I asked.

"Yes," she answered with a dark smile. "You forget how much we dislike him."

We trailed after the dogs and it wasn't long before Gwynn lifted a paw and then resumed his sniffing, more fiercely this time.

"He's got the scent," Isabeau murmured.

"Good. Let's go kick some ass," Quinn said, withdrawing a stake from the leather strap across his chest.

"Hey, give me one of those." I took one from Connor as well and handed it to Isabeau. She'd tossed the broken lilac branch into the bushes earlier.

"Wait," Isabeau said repressively as we jogged after the dogs. "We need a plan."

"We find them, kill the bastards, rescue our parents," Quinn explained.

"You can't just run in there and hope Montmartre trips on his own stake," Isabeau said. "He's really good at this sort of thing. He's been doing it for centuries and we . . . haven't. And there's only six of us, and most of us are newborn. Once the sun comes up, he can keep fighting. We can't."

"We only need to distract him," Solange insisted. "Give Mom and Dad and the others a chance to fight back."

"That's something," Isabeau agreed. "But it's not enough. We've got the dogs," she said as we picked up speed. "I'll call the Hounds with directions once we know where they are and they might be able to get to us in time."

"We can't wait," Quinn argued.

"I know that. We can't just barge in either," she insisted. "But maybe we can use one of their own tricks against them. How's your balance?"

We looked at her like she'd lost her mind.

"Our balance? We're not joining the circus here."

"Just listen. We send the dogs in and then we follow, but from up high. If we can move from tree to tree, we'll have an advantage and the element of surprise."

"I haven't swung from a trapeze lately," Quinn said dryly, but he was grinning. "But I'll damn well learn fast. You're sneaky and vicious, Isabeau," he added. "I think I like you."

"I think they're heading to the clearing off the fens." Connor frowned down at the GPS on his phone. "I'm sending the coordinates to everyone we know right now."

"Send them to Magda too." Isabeau rattled off her number. Two soft short whistles had the dogs moving more silently, ears perked.

"Nearly there," Connor said.

"Let's climb," she suggested. Quinn and Nicholas went wide, circling to the other side of the clearing. I could smell the Host and their victims now, the forest drenched in pheromones and bloodlust. Fangs extended all around. Isabeau's hadn't retracted since we'd been ambushed. She shimmied up an elm tree, startling a squirrel into a hole in the trunk. She moved lightly along a high branch, dropping down onto a nearby oak branch and hopping up to another elm.

We used a curtain of leaves to hide as we assessed the situation down below. An outer circle of Host guards in their brown leather patrolled with crossbows. We had managed to avoid their notice so far. There were more just inside the clearing and a clump of them in the center where Montmartre stood, an arrow pointed at Mom's chest. Dad was snarling, on his knees, a sword tip grazing his jugular. Blood dripped from a gash on his temple. Sebastian and

Marcus stood very still. Montmartre was smiling pleasantly. Grey-haven waited behind him impatiently. I wished I had a crossbow of my own.

But that would have to wait.

"*Merde*," Isabeau snapped. "You're not the only Drake with a martyr complex."

Solange strolled into the meadow, muffled curses shivering in the treetops as Nicholas, Quinn, and Connor struggled not to give themselves away. Only Isabeau's hand on my arm stopped me from launching out of the tree.

"Montmartre," Solange called out, swinging the crown from her fingertips, the faint moonlight glimmering on the diamonds. "Let's make a trade."

Chapter 24

Isabeau

Montmartre looked up, smile widening. "Solange, darling. So glad to see you've recovered."

Helena closed her eyes briefly. "Solange, no."

"Stay the hell away from my daughter," Liam added, seething. Montmartre flicked his hand dismissively. Solange took another step forward, out of the protection of the sheltering trees.

"Little idiot." Logan seethed. "The last time she gave herself up for us, she nearly got killed."

"I knew you'd come to your senses," Montmartre told her pleasantly, his long hair hanging down his back.

"If you let my family go unharmed," she said, fisting her hands to hide the trembling of her fingers, "I'll stay with you."

"The hell you will," Logan yelled, finally swinging into the clearing. His brothers followed suit, like deranged monkeys. I barely had time to whistle the dogs into an attack.

Every single one of the Drake brothers was insane.

We had no idea if the Hounds were close enough to help us; we had barely enough weapons between us and a traitor below.

What was a lady to do?

I leaped into the fray, of course.

I staked a guard as I landed and she plumed into dust. I caught her sword before it fell in the grass with her empty clothes. I drove the bottle shard smeared with Montmartre's blood into the ground. The *Hel-Blar* would follow its scent to us. They would make things worse, no doubt about that, but they'd attack Montmartre and the Host at least as much as they'd attack us.

The Host didn't hesitate, didn't even wait for orders. Helena didn't hesitate either. The very second Montmartre glanced at her daughter, she kicked the crossbow out of his hand. She couldn't do much more than that; there were too many of them. Liam roared to his feet, Sebastian and Marcus spun to fight their captors. The dogs growled and bit their way through the Host. Nicholas and Connor were fighting back-to-back and Quinn was flipping his way to Solange's side. Greyhaven was in the middle of it all with wildflowers incongruously around his knees. I saw him open his cell phone and bark a terse command into it. There were too many battle sounds to hear him properly but I could read his lips. *It's time.*

He was calling his men for the coup.

And then suddenly that was the least of our worries.

The smell of mushrooms hit us first, and one of the dogs let out a howl-growl that warned of the *Hel-Blar*.

And then they were everywhere, like blue beetles eating through everything in their path.

Calling them had seemed like a good idea at the time.

Well, not precisely a good idea, so much as the only one we had.

But it wasn't enough.

Not nearly.

I fought my way toward Logan, using sword and stake. Charlemagne stayed close, savaging the knee of a Host who got too close. He stayed down, clutching his leg. I jumped over him, staked another Host, and got stabbed in the left arm for my troubles.

"Logan," I called.

His eyes narrowed on my wound. "You're hurt, damn it."

I shrugged, causing more blood to trickle down my forearm. He ducked a stake, grabbed me, and knocked me down as an arrow grazed over our heads.

"I need to dreamwalk," I told him.

"What, *now?*"

"We can't win, not like this."

"Damn," he said, but I knew he agreed with me. "There." He pointed to a thick nest of ferns. I rolled into them, lying still until the fronds draped over me. I wasn't completely hidden but it was the best we could reasonably expect. Charlemagne stood over my head. Logan stood at my feet.

"Hurry up," he grunted, staking a *Hel-Blar* that snapped his jaws at us.

I closed my eyes, which was an act of will in itself; lying still and vulnerable like this while a battle raged around me was the hardest thing I'd done, nearly as difficult as abandoning my vengeance.

I took three deep breaths, counted them slowly, focused intently on the sensation of air my lungs didn't need; it was the ritual of it that mattered. I chanted the ancient words, then sat up, leaving my body behind lying scarred and eerily still in the ferns.

Blood soaked silver over the grass, ashes gathered on wildflower petals and the exposed roots of knobbly oak trees. The Drakes had only brought three guards with them when they'd left the caves for home and two of them had already been turned to dust. The third was howling, her pale skin and hair practically glowing.

Montmartre stalked toward Solange. Connor tried to block him and was tossed into Nicholas. They both landed hard, nearly knocking Marcus down in the process. Solange, wild-eyed, threw her last stake. It went wide and only clipped Montmartre's collar. She flung the crown at his head, it was all she had left.

"For the last time, I don't want the damn crown," she yelled.

"You can stop all this fighting," he said. "If you come with me now."

"Don't you dare, Solange Rose," Helena bellowed. "He can't control the *Hel-Blar* and he sure as hell doesn't keep his word."

"And haven't we been through this before?" Quinn grunted, punching his fist into a Host eyeball. "You couldn't have her last week and you can't have her now."

We were running out of time.

I floated over the meadow and forced the energy of my glowing spirit out into the air, visualized it turning to mist and clinging to the Host and the *Hel-Blar*, choking Greyhaven with a glitter of sunlight. I visualized it so hard even my astral body dripped sweat. I was using my own energy, pushing and pushing until I was sick with exhaustion and fog snaked into the clearing. I sent it toward our enemies, gritting my astral teeth at the pain lancing through both my bodies. I'd never been able to sustain the mist for long periods of time before—it was too advanced, too draining. No help for it.

"What the hell is this?" Greyhaven batted at the mist as it clung to him. It wasn't thick enough yet, he could still see the others. For this to work properly, soon we would see the Host but they wouldn't see us.

At least Montmartre's advance on Solange had been delayed, not just by the strange mist, but also by the *Hel-Blar*, maddened by his scent. Logan was tiring but he refused to give in. I knew he'd protect me until he was dust. I had no intention of letting that happen. I had to get back into my body, and soon.

But first I needed to create just a little more mist. The light cord linking my spirit to myself dimmed and I knew the longer I stayed incorporeal and using this much magical energy, the more I risked being stranded like this forever. I added just a little more mist and was talking myself into making a little more when I noticed the glitter of fireflies between the branches and all around us.

Not fireflies.

Hounds.

To my spirit-sight they came through the trees like sparks of light, like firecrackers exploding.

But it was too early to celebrate.

Because from the other direction, I could see the red-tinged sparks that were Greyhaven's men's auras, also closing in. I couldn't separate magical vision from ordinary vision in this state. Auras shifted and glowed and sparked, like a watercolor wash over a charcoal sketch.

"Incoming!" Liam shouted grimly. "Who the hell are these guys?"

"Greyhaven's trying a hostile takeover," Logan shouted.

"What, *now?*"

The Host still loyal to Montmartre were stunned into pausing, seeing some of their brothers turn to help the newcomers against them. The unexpected coup rattled them.

It was just enough of an advantage for our side. We might not all die horribly after all.

I saw the exact moment when Greyhaven noticed Logan, when he saw my arm hanging limp out of the ferns.

He was faster than I was.

He flung a stake at Logan and caught him just next to his heart. Logan stumbled, pain twisting his pretty face. Blood seeped through his fingers, staining his shirt. He'd be mad about the damage to his clothes later.

If he survived the night.

He'd damn well better survive, since he'd forced me to.

I flung myself at my body but I was so tired, it was like moving through honey. I didn't realize I was screaming until Magda looked up.

Greyhaven had reached Logan, who was fumbling with wet fingers for a stake. The one in his chest was still there, stuck in bone and muscle. Charlemagne growled, lips quivering. Greyhaven bared his own fangs and reached out, quick as a wasp, to shove at the stake already piercing Logan. He drove it deeper. Logan screamed. Greyhaven backhanded him hard enough to knock him off his feet. Logan shook his head, groaning, and tried to crawl between Greyhaven and my defenseless body.

And I could only hover uselessly, too slow to stop Greyhaven from killing me again.

And Logan.

That thought alone was enough to galvanize me into action.

But it was too late. Greyhaven's sword flashed as he kicked the ferns aside, exposing me completely. Charlemagne sprung but Greyhaven was a blur of tailored suit and sword.

If he hurt my dog I'd find a way to kill him twice.

Magda was faster than all of us.

Her sword blocked Greyhaven's just as it cut through a lacy frond, skimming the chain mail over my heart.

"She's my kill," Greyhaven spat.

"Go to hell."

Her eyes met mine as I floated above them. And then she drove her sword through Greyhaven's heart, twisted, and stepped back.

Greyhaven had time to look surprised and then he broke apart into ashes. One of his men howled.

Logan crawled to my side, yanking the stake out of his flesh with a savage curse.

The Hounds descended at the same time and at some signal from Finn, they fell into formation, dispatching Host and *Hel-Blar*, and Greyhaven's men, all stumbling blindly in the mist. The Host had the added difficulty of fighting their own turncoat brothers. I tried to pull some of the mist away from the Hounds and the Drakes but I was too weak.

"Retreat!" Liam shouted at his family. "That's an order!"

Montmartre flung orders but his Host were too far away to help him. He bumped into Helena, mostly by chance, just as she was drawing her arm back to stake a *Hel-Blar*. He caught her hand and jerked his other arm around her throat, fangs descending. She was caught by surprise, twisted at a strange angle, half-obscured by mist. Everyone was too busy, too wounded, or too far to help her.

Except Solange.

She elbowed Montmartre in the ear, hard enough to snap his head to the side. He turned, snarling. But she was already scooping the discarded crown out of the ash-covered grass.

Solange drove the broken spokes through his back, right over his heart. It wasn't enough to pierce his heart entirely, snapping off in his shoulder. Helena spun him around and finished the job, shoving a stake through his chest.

He howled and disintegrated, leaving mother and daughter staring at each other with dusty boots.

Quinn gave a bark of triumphant laughter and Magda spun like a mad fairy, flinging stakes from her hands. The Host, seeing their leader dispatched, stumbled, looking for escape.

And I still wasn't inside my body.

I'd stayed too long.

The mist was thinning, the battle was breaking apart, and I hovered over myself as if a pane of glass barred my return. The veins under my skin looked too pronounced, my cheekbones too harsh. My scars were like satin. I was disoriented, dizzy.

I wasn't strong enough to control the magic.

It was controlling me.

The sun rose, sending arrows of light between the trees. The *Hel-Blar* howled, seeking shelter. The Host dispersed. Logan scooped me up, running through the ferns. Birds began their morning song. The sky turned the color of opal. Liam pushed his family forward as Helena dove for a wooden door hidden under the brush. Sebastian was carrying Solange, who, being the youngest, had already passed out. My spirit followed behind them, too slow, watching my body get carried farther out of reach.

The Drakes dropped into the tunnel, one by one. Logan handed me down to one of his brothers as blood still seeped from his wound. I felt his mouth brush my ear.

"Isabeau." He sounded frantic, furious. "Isabeau," he said again. "Isabeau!"

He'd remembered what I'd told him about repeating a name to return a spirit to its body.

I'd have kissed him if I could have.

I landed so suddenly and so violently that I twitched uncontrollably, eyes rolling back in my head.

EPILOGUE

Logan

The next night I found Isabeau sitting on the roof of the farmhouse, watching the stars come out over the forest. She still wore her tunic dress, a little torn at the hem but wiped clean of mud. I couldn't help but remember the vision of her running along the roofs of Paris in her stolen coat. I stretched out next to her on the shingles that still retained the heat of the day. She wouldn't look at me, as if she didn't quite know how to be around me. I was going to take that as a good sign.

"How are you feeling?" I asked. Her veins were still unnaturally blue, her eyes red; side effects of nearly burning herself up with magic.

"*Ça va*," she replied. "Thank you," she added, so formally she actually winced afterward.

I smiled a little. "That was some trick with the mist."

She nodded. "There is so much we don't know yet about our magic. I wasn't sure I could work that spell. I certainly couldn't unwork it once I'd started. I'd have been trapped in spirit form if it weren't for you."

"Are you sorry you didn't get to kill Greyhaven yourself?" I asked quietly.

She considered that and finally shook her head slowly. "No. I guess that doesn't make me much of a warrior, does it?"

"I wouldn't say that." I snorted. "Dogs and magic mists are a hell of a battle strategy." I reached for her hand, weaving my fingers through hers. "You're still staying for the coronation?"

"*Oui.*"

I looked at her. She sighed a little. "How do you do that?"

"Do what?"

"No one else in the world has ever seen me the way you have, not even Kala. You saw what I was. Before." I knew she was remembering those rooftops too. "And yet you still look at me as if I matter, as if I'm somehow precious."

"You *are* precious," I insisted. "Stubborn and secretive and independent to a fault, but precious."

"Oh."

I thought she might be blushing. "I love you, Isabeau."

She was definitely blushing now. She blinked at me. I just stared back patiently. "Come on, the bones said we're meant for each other," I reminded her.

"Who told you that?"

"Magda. She doesn't hate me quite as much as she used to."

"Oh."

I smiled. "Don't be scared, Isabeau."

"I'm not scared," she insisted indignantly.

"Oh, please. One little 'I love you' has you all freaked out. No sword or stake or slavering dog-beast can get you that pale and stiff."

She seemed to fight a short battle inside herself, one I could only watch. I didn't have the weapons to help her. Only she had them.

"You have a point, I suppose." She unfisted her hands. "And what is a warrior but someone who faces her fears and defeats them?" She swallowed. "*Je . . .*" She swallowed again. "*Je t'aime.*"

I'd never known the kind of bone-deep satisfaction I knew right then and there. I lifted our joined hands to my mouth, kissing her knuckles.

"That wasn't so hard, was it?" I asked hoarsely.

She smiled. "I suppose not."

She lay back down next to me, our sides touching, her hair fluttering over my arm, smelling like leaves and berries. We lay under the stars for a long time.

"Will you visit me in the caves?" she whispered finally. "After the ceremonies and the council meetings are through?"

"Of course."

"Even though everyone will disapprove?"

I pushed up on my elbow. Her eyes were so green they nearly glowed. "I couldn't care less what everyone else thinks." I lowered my head, my mouth hovering over hers. "Besides . . . ," I grinned slowly. "Think of it as intertribal negotiations."

She touched my jaw, smiling back, softly, lightly. "As handmaiden, it *is* my duty to foster a good relationship between the Cwn Mamau and the royal family."

"Exactly." I closed the last inch between us and kissed her.

And when she kissed me back we weren't a prince and a handmaiden, weren't Drake and Hound, weren't anything or anyone but Logan and Isabeau. Together.

ALYXANDRA HARVEY studied creative writing and literature at York University and has had her poetry published in magazines. She likes lattes, chocolate, and tattoos and lives in an old Victorian farmhouse in Ontario, Canada, with her husband and three dogs.

www.alyxandraharvey.com
www.thedrakechronicles.com

Look out for the sensational next
instalment in the

DRAKE CHRONICLES

Out for
Blood

New from Alyxandra Harvey
in November 2010